"Just for tonight could we pretend that we're not who we are?"

Confused, Dex tried to read her expression for some hint of what she was thinking. "I don't know what you mean."

"Let's pretend you're not Ty Cooper, the rancher who loves nothing more than raising cattle. That I'm not Leanne Watley, struggling dude rancher. And that our parents haven't tried to marry us off for years. Let's just be two people who want to have a nice time together for one evening. Just one night," she added softly.

"We can do that." He stared directly into her eyes, hunger roaring inside him. At that moment he would have given anything to *really* have her for one night. "Just for tonight."

He wondered if Miss Leanne Watley had any idea how close to the edge she'd pushed him. It would take nothing short of a miracle to keep him from crossing the line tonight.

Dear Reader,

Millionaire. Prince. Secret agent. Doctor. If any—or all—
of these men strike your fancy, well…you're in luck! These
fabulous guys are waiting for you in the pages of this
month's offerings from Harlequin American Romance.

His best friend's request to father her child leads
millionaire Gabe Deveraux to offer a bold marriage
proposal in *My Secret Wife* by Cathy Gillen Thacker,
the latest installment of THE DEVERAUX LEGACY
series. A royal request makes Prince Jace Carradigne
heir to a throne—and in search of his missing fiancée—
in Mindy Neff's *The Inconveniently Engaged Prince*, part
of our ongoing series THE CARRADIGNES: AMERICAN
ROYALTY. (And there are royals galore to be found
when the series comes to a sensational ending in
Heir to the Throne, a special two-in-one collection by
Kasey Michaels and Carolyn Davidson, available next
month wherever Harlequin books are sold.)

Kids, kangaroos and a kindhearted woman are all
in a day's work for cool and collected secret agent
Mike Wheeler in *Secret Service Dad*, the second book in
Mollie Molay's GROOMS IN UNIFORM series. And a big-
city doctor attempts to hide his true identity—and his
affections—for a Montana beauty in *The Doctor Wore Boots*
by Debra Webb, the conclusion to the TRADING PLACES
duo.

So be sure to catch all of these wonderful men this
month—and every month—as you enjoy their wonderful
love stories from Harlequin American Romance.

Happy reading,

Melissa Jeglinski
Associate Senior Editor
Harlequin American Romance

THE DOCTOR WORE BOOTS

Debra Webb

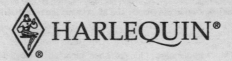

HARLEQUIN®

TORONTO • NEW YORK • LONDON
AMSTERDAM • PARIS • SYDNEY • HAMBURG
STOCKHOLM • ATHENS • TOKYO • MILAN • MADRID
PRAGUE • WARSAW • BUDAPEST • AUCKLAND

Special thanks to Alitza Wellstead
for always being there when I call.
This one is for you, Alitza!

ISBN 0-373-16948-5

THE DOCTOR WORE BOOTS

This edition published by arrangement with Harlequin Books S.A.

® and TM are trademarks of the publisher. Trademarks indicated with
® are registered in the United States Patent and Trademark Office, the
Canadian Trade Marks Office and in other countries.

Visit us at www.eHarlequin.com

Printed in U.S.A.

ABOUT THE AUTHOR

Debra Webb was born in Scottsboro, Alabama, to parents who taught her that anything is possible if you want it badly enough. She began writing at age nine. Eventually she met and married the man of her dreams and tried some other occupations, including selling vacuum cleaners and working in a factory, a day-care center, a hospital and a department store. When her husband joined the military, they moved to Berlin, Germany, and Debra became a secretary in the commanding general's office. By 1985 they were back in the States, and finally moved to Tennessee, to a small town where everyone knows everyone else. With the support of her husband and two beautiful daughters, Debra took up writing again, looking to mystery and movies for inspiration. In 1998 her dream of writing for Harlequin came true. You can write to Debra with your comments at P.O. Box 64, Huntland, Tennessee 37345.

Books by Debra Webb

HARLEQUIN AMERICAN ROMANCE
864—LONGWALKER'S CHILD
935—THE MARRIAGE PRESCRIPTION*
948—THE DOCTOR WORE BOOTS

HARLEQUIN INTRIGUE
583—SAFE BY HIS SIDE*
597—THE BODYGUARD'S BABY*
610—PROTECTIVE CUSTODY*
634—SPECIAL ASSIGNMENT: BABY
646—SOLITARY SOLDIER*
659—PERSONAL PROTECTOR*
671—PHYSICAL EVIDENCE*
683—CONTRACT BRIDE*

*Colby Agency

Dex Montgomery's Cheat Sheet:
How To Be Ty Cooper

1. Wear worn jeans and cowboy boots.

2. Figure out which brother is Chad and which is Court.

3. Stop staring at Leanne Watley.

4. Remember to wear your Stetson.

5. Learn how to ride a horse.

6. Use your left hand, not your right.

7. Stop your little niece Angelica from revealing the truth.

8. Try not to fantasize about the beautiful Leanne....

Pre-Prologue

Once upon a time there was a beautiful young girl and a handsome young boy who fell deeply in love. But, alas, their families were at odds. So, determined to keep the two apart, the young boy's family took him and moved far, far away.

Many years later, when they were all grown up, the young man and the young woman found each other once more. Unwilling to risk separation again, they married swiftly before either of their families could object. As expected, many hurtful words were spoken, much damage was done, but love prevailed. Nothing could tear the loving couple apart.

To add to their happiness, less than one year later they were blessed with a perfect set of twin boys. The lovely young couple was so very happy at last. But that happiness was short-lived. Fate intervened in the form of a fatal car crash.

Both families were devastated. All that remained of their only children were the twin grandsons. A fierce custody battle ensued, widening the rift. Finally, a judge made the only fair decision he felt was possible; he gave each set of grandparents one of the twins. Due to the extreme hostility between the families, he ordered that all future contact be limited until they learned to get along. Taking the judge's words too much to heart, the estranged families, with their respective namesakes in tow, went their separate ways and never looked back.

Until now.

Prologue

Dex Montgomery allowed his briefcase to collapse to the floor next to the only empty table in the crowded bar. He jerked at his tie and dropped into a chair, completely disgusted.

Two hours. His flight was delayed for *two hours*. What was he supposed to do for two hours?

"Are you ready to order, sir?"

Dex heaved a sigh fraught with equal measures of impatience and frustration and looked up at the waitress watching him expectantly.

"Scotch," he told her. "No water. And make it a double."

She nodded and headed in the direction of the bar, weaving her way through the throngs of occupied tables and pausing occasionally to take another customer's order.

Glancing at his watch, Dex considered whether or not to call in and inform his grandfather of the delay. He definitely wouldn't make this afternoon's meeting of the board. Dex frowned. Montgomery men had no tolerance for delays. There was little he could do about it, however. The old man would simply have to fend for himself. His frown relaxed a bit with that thought. Charles Dexter Montgomery, Senior, was getting a little soft anyway. Sparring with the sharks who made up the board of M3I would be good for him.

Considering the boring financial conference Dex had just endured, it was only fair. This was the third conference he'd attended in the last two months. He was sick of hearing how M3I could improve its profit margin. Dex clenched his jaw. Modern Medical Maintenance, Inc., affectionately known as M3I, maintained a very healthy profit margin. Dex and his grandfather saw to that. They'd started with a single facility in Atlanta and had built a medical empire. M3I now consisted of a chain of cutting-edge facilities throughout the Southeast. The business was focused on providing quality medical care and making a profit.

Not necessarily in that order.

"Anything else?" The waitress placed the drink in front of him and smiled. Not a thank-you-for-your-patronage kind of smile, but one that became a predatory gleam in her eyes. She was flirting.

"No, thank you." He paid the lady and turned his attention to his drink. He didn't need a flirtatious waitress and he damn sure didn't need two hours in a bar.

He needed work.

Dex almost laughed out loud at that one. What he did wasn't work, it was choreography. He led a well-rehearsed dance to the sound of money changing hands. The medical degree and license he held were mere icing on the cake of the distinguished position as chairman of the board. Dr. Dexter Montgomery. It had the right ring to it even if it wasn't for practicing medicine. No doctor with the Montgomery name would dare sully his hands treating patients. Not when there was money to be made.

Dex stopped himself. He always got this way when he spent any length of time away from the office. That's why he all but lived at the office. Work was his life. He knew nothing else, didn't even have a hobby. And why should he? He had plans. Plans that didn't include silly, sentimental musings.

"To profit margins," he muttered and downed a hefty gulp of Scotch.

The hair on the back of his neck suddenly stood on end. Frowning again, he tilted his head left then right, stretching to relieve some of the tension. But that little niggling sensation of being watched just wouldn't go away. He glanced around the room, then did a double-take. A couple of tables away a man, his cowboy hat on the table before him, sat, seemingly paralyzed, the glass in his hand halfway to his mouth.

Dex registered surprise first…then incredulity. The cowboy was dressed differently than he was, no Armani or Cardin, but he looked exactly the same. Same thick dark hair, cropped short. Maybe his was a fraction longer. Same dark eyes…same square jaw… same…everything.

Dex pushed to his feet, the legs of his chair scraping across the tiled floor. Before he had the good sense to stop himself and think about what he was doing he'd crossed to the man's table, passed his drink to his left hand and extended his right. "Dex Montgomery," he said numbly.

Apparently shocked himself, the cowboy stared first at Dex's hand, then at him. "Ty Cooper," he responded stiffly. His callused hand closed over Dex's. The contact was brief but something passed between them. Some strange energy that felt alien but somehow oddly familiar.

Dex shook his head in question. "Who…? How…?" This was surreal. The man didn't just resemble him—he looked exactly like him.

Apparently at a loss himself, Ty gestured to the empty chair on the opposite side of the small table. "Maybe you'd better have a seat."

Dumbfounded, Dex complied. "This isn't possible. I mean…" He shook his head again. "I'm a doctor and even I'm at a loss for an explanation." This couldn't be. It was like looking into a mirror. It was bizarre.

The other man scrubbed a hand over his chin. "You're right, partner. It's a little weird looking at your reflection in another man's face. Maybe we're related somehow?" He laughed nervously. "You know, distantly. Identical cousins or something."

Dex lifted one shoulder, then let it fall. "That's possible, I suppose." A memory pinged him. "Did you say Cooper?" he asked, almost hesitantly.

Ty nodded. "Of Rolling Bend, Montana. We have a cattle ranch called the—"

"Rolling Bend, Montana?" A chunk of ice formed in Dex's stomach.

"Yeah." Ty swallowed hard. "You know the place?"

Dex's gaze settled fully onto his. *He* couldn't believe what he was about to say. "My mother's name was Tara Cooper. She was born in Rolling Bend."

Ty signaled the passing waitress. "Ma'am, we're gonna need another round here," he said, his voice hollow.

She glanced at Dex, then started visibly when her gaze landed back on Ty. "Doubles for doubles," she said with a giggle. "Are you guys twins or something?"

Dex glared at her and she scurried away. Ty leaned forward as if what he had to say was too unbelievable to utter out loud. "Tara Cooper was *my* mother."

A choked sound, not quite a laugh, burst from Dex. "But my mother died when I was three months old."

"My birth date is May 21, 1970," Ty countered. "My mother died in an accident with my father when *I* was three months old."

"Oh yeah? Well, so did mine. But I don't have any siblings," Dex argued, unable to comprehend what he could see with his own eyes.

"Neither do I—well, except for my adopted brothers."

Dex gestured vaguely. "Maybe there were two Tara Coopers in Rolling Bend?"

Ty moved his head slowly from side to side. "We're the only Cooper clan in that neck of the woods."

"I'm certain there's some reasonable explanation," Dex suggested. Adrenaline pulsed through his veins making his heart pound. This man couldn't be his brother. That was impossible.

"There's an explanation all right," Ty said flatly. "We've been had."

THREE HOURS and too many drinks to remember later, Dex had concluded the only reasonable explanation.

Ty Cooper was not only his brother, but his identical twin. They had both missed their scheduled flights home, but neither cared.

The stories of their parents' whirlwind courtship, marriage and tragic deaths matched down to the dates. Ty had been told, as had Dex, that he had no other family. Dex could just imagine the reaction of his grandfather when his only son had married a rancher's daughter. Dex had only been told his mother's name, little else.

"What I want to know," Ty said, his speech a little slower, thicker, "is how the hell did they decide who would take who?"

For one long moment the two just looked at each other. Dex wondered briefly what his life would have been like if he'd been chosen by the other set of grandparents, but he couldn't begin to imagine. Considering his grandfather Montgomery's penchant for absolute control, Dex couldn't help thinking how the old man would react when he found out that Dex had learned the truth. He had no doubt that his grandfather was the mastermind behind this whole scheme.

"We should show up together and stage a confrontation," Dex commented dryly before draining his glass.

Ty grinned. "You may have something there." Those unnervingly familiar dark eyes twinkled with mischief now. "I say we give 'em a taste of their own medicine."

A flash of concern found its way through the warm, Scotch-induced haze now cloaking Dex. "What do you have in mind?"

Ty motioned to the waitress and then pointed to their empty glasses once more. "I'm talking about trading places, brother. For just a little while," he added quickly. "Just long enough to teach our families a lesson."

Dex hesitated at first, then a smile slid across his face. "Oh, that's good. All we have to do is bring each other up to speed on how to act and what to do." He flared his hands and inclined his head in a gesture of nonchalance. "It's simple on my end. You leave the business decisions to the old man. I have a secretary and a financial advisor who take care of things at the office. They'll keep you straight on the day-to-day schedule." He paused, considering. "If a problem does come up and you need to make a financial decision on your own, use your own discretion. You *are* a Montgomery."

"Same here," Ty assured him. "I have two adopted brothers. Between them and the ranch hands, they can handle things at the Circle C. It'll be good for both of us. We can get to know the rest of our family."

Dex nodded, though he was more concerned at the moment with teaching his grandfather a lesson than anything else. He noted the time. "All right, then," he said. "We have ninety minutes before our flights leave for our respective destinations. Let's do it."

Ty folded his arms over his chest. "You go first. I have a feeling your folks are a lot more complicated than mine."

Dex didn't bother to tell him that *complicated* was not the word he was looking for, instead he told Ty Cooper everything he would need to know in order to play Dexter Montgomery for just a little while.

Chapter One

What the devil had he done?

Reality crashed down around Dex Montgomery as he stood in the designated pick-up area at Gallatin Field Airport in Bozeman, Montana. Ty had told him where to wait for his ride, and someone from the Cooper clan would pick him up.

Dex swallowed hard, his head aching from one Scotch too many. It was the first time in his entire life he could recall having too much to drink and a hangover all in the same afternoon. But now, as the grim reality of his actions settled around him, he knew today was not like any other he'd experienced in his thirty-two years. He doubted his life would ever be the same again.

The Gucci briefcase, Louis Vuitton garment bag, and state-of-the-art cellular phone he'd left home with just four days ago were now in the possession of a virtual stranger. A stranger who was his twin brother, who, in another hour or so, would be climbing into *his* limo and riding to *his* home to meet *his* family.

What the hell was *he* doing here?

Dex dropped the army-style duffel bag belonging

to Ty Cooper to the ground. He tugged at the collar of the unstarched shirt he now wore and attempted to straighten the off-the-rack jacket. It was very obvious to Dex that his brother had absolutely no taste in clothing. The jeans were criminally worn and far too tight for comfort. The boots—Dex shook his head— had definitely seen better days. Though he doubted that even in mint condition he would have cared for the unnaturally high-arched footwear. He tried not to think about the cowboy hat perched atop his head. The urge to remove it was almost more than he could restrain.

Didn't cowboys keep their hats on at all times?

What had possessed him to change clothes with another man, brother or not, in an airport rest room?

Temporary insanity. It was the only possible explanation. Stress had finally taken its toll. George, his valet, friend and confidant, had warned him that he was pushing too hard, working far too many hours. But Dex had refused to listen. He had to prove his worth, couldn't risk disappointing his grandfather. He was thirty-two, for Pete's sake. He had mountains to climb and oceans to cross. His mark to make.

He had lost his mind. Here he stood, in the middle of nowhere, when he should be dictating correspondence, crunching numbers, planning takeovers. His grandfather counted on him, trusted him unconditionally.

He couldn't do this.

One telephone call would end this ruse here and now.

Dex grabbed the bag he'd abandoned on the ground and pivoted toward the airport entrance. This was a bad idea. Surely there would be another flight out of here sometime tonight. At the moment he really didn't care where it was going, as long as it took him back to a more recognizable form of civilization.

"Ty!"

A vehicle screeched to a halt behind him.

"Ty! Over here!" a feminine voice shouted.

Dex froze. *Ty.* His transportation had arrived. Dex swore under his breath. He should just keep walking without looking back. But then he'd never know...

Slowly, his head throbbing with frustration and the lingering effects of alcohol, he turned and faced step two of his self-created nightmare.

A young woman waved from behind the wheel of an old pickup truck. "Sorry you had to wait!" she called. She leaned across the seat and opened the passenger-side door. "I didn't know until an hour ago that I would be coming to pick you up."

Blond hair, blue eyes—she was very young, twenty-two or three maybe. Dex frowned, searching his memory banks for the name that went with the face. Leanne. Leanne Watley. Neighbor. Family friend. The kid-sister type, Ty had said.

"I got here as fast as I could," she hastened to add when he continued to simply stare at her. "Come on. Gran's holding supper until I get you home. They've got a big celebration planned for your return."

Somehow his feet moved. Dex wasn't exactly sure how he managed the monumental task considering his brain felt paralyzed with uncertainty, but he took the necessary steps just the same.

He slid onto the ragged bench seat and awkwardly settled the big duffel onto his lap. He couldn't imagine what possessed people to drive vehicles like this. There was no place to put anything. And the seat was most uncomfortable.

Leanne laughed. "You can put that in the back. It's not raining."

The back. "Of course." His face heated. He wasn't usually so inept. As he climbed out of the vehicle, Dex hoped she couldn't see the level of disorientation afflicting him. His movements felt jerky, his ability to think nonexistent. He placed the worn bag into the bed of the truck and settled back into the passenger seat. He closed the door and offered her a strained smile. "Thank you."

She frowned, just the slightest creasing of her smooth brow. "I guess you're really tired. I'm sorry you had to wait for a ride."

"Your delayed arrival was completely understandable," he assured her. "Considering the unexpected change in my return itinerary, your reaction time was quite acceptable."

Her eyes widened with something that looked very much like worry. "Are you all right, Ty? You sound a little…strange."

Dex realized his mistake immediately. He was Ty Cooper now. Looking like him wasn't enough, he had to speak and act like him as well.

"Jet lag," he offered as much to his surprise as to hers. Could one actually acquire jet lag on a short jaunt that only crossed one time zone?

She nodded. "Oh."

By the time they left Bozeman behind, the sick feeling in the pit of Dex's stomach had escalated to a near-intolerable level. He shifted restlessly, peering out the window. How long before they would reach the ranch? How could he possibly fool Ty's grandparents? This would never work. He should just demand that she turn around right now and take him back to the airport. Instead, he reviewed over and over again the information Ty had relayed to him regarding his family and the layout of the ranch. He reminded himself again to use his left hand as much as possible. Ty was a lefty.

"How'd the meeting with those investors go?" she asked, breaking the long, awkward silence.

Dex jerked back to attention. "Excuse me?"

"Are you sure you're feeling all right?" She looked at him with that genuine concern again.

"Yes, yes," he assured her. "I'm fine. The meeting went…was okay…I guess." He'd forgotten to ask Ty why he was in Chicago. She'd said investors. "I won't know anything for a few days," he added for good measure. That was typical. Investors made lots of promises, but the real story was revealed much more slowly. If Ty had begun some sort of deal, only time would tell if it was a good one or not.

Leanne sighed. "That's too bad. I know you were hoping to have news when you got back."

"Yes." He cleared his throat. "Yeah. I was."

He glanced at the young woman behind the wheel. What was she thinking? Had she seen through him already? Worry twisted inside him. If he couldn't get through a few simple questions from a neighbor without making her suspicious, how on earth would he fool the Coopers?

"I know how much this deal means to you, Ty," she went on, worry weighting her voice. "But maybe it's like your pa said. Maybe you'll just have to be happy with things the way they are. It's not like you don't have enough buyers to keep your ranch going. The Circle C has provided high-quality beef to its customers for three generations now.''

The cattle market. So that was the kind of investors Ty had gone to the city to meet. Dex was somewhat familiar with the distressed American market. Foreign beef had made a big comeback in the United States recently, a huge surge from the past couple of years when disease had wrought such devastation for European countries. Was Ty trying to increase the reach of his own ranch's production? That sounded reasonable to Dex. He'd have to ask Ty about that or risk making a wrong step.

"I'd like to go to Chicago sometime," Leanne said wistfully, drawing Dex's attention in her direction. She huffed, her gaze steady on the endless ribbon of blacktop that lay before them. "I've never even been out of the state. I don't know why I'm fretting over Chicago. I doubt I'll ever be going there.''

Dex looked at her then, really looked at her. She was quite attractive. She wore no makeup as far as he could tell, but she didn't need any. She looked vibrant, healthy. That notion sent the corners of his mouth tilting upward for some reason he couldn't understand. She was nothing like the women he knew. Oh, and young. He almost asked her age, but caught himself just in time. Ty would know how old she was. Young, that was certain. Too damned young.

"You should go sometime," he suggested. "Life is short, make the most of it.''

"I don't see that happening," she said regretfully.

Her gaze locked onto his as she slowed to make a right turn onto a gravel road. In that infinitesimal moment something electric passed between them. Startled, she looked away.

Startled himself, Dex gave his head a little shake. What the hell was that? He was disoriented, that's all. He'd be fine as soon as he—

As soon as he what? There was no way he was going to be fine. He was in the middle of nowhere with strangers. Worst of all he was pretending to be someone he'd only just met.

This whole idea had sounded much more doable before he'd sobered up.

Miles of nothing stretched before him as well as behind him. In the time since they'd left the city of Bozeman, they had encountered highway and mountains, nothing more.

A blue sky, fading slowly into dusk, looked almost low enough to touch. Dex couldn't recall ever feeling this close to the heavens before. He scrubbed a hand over his face. The disorientation was clearly turning to delusions. This was bad. Very bad.

She turned right again, this time onto a long winding dirt road. The sun barely hovered above the mountaintops in the distance. Acres and acres of fenced pasture yawned on either side of the rough road. Cattle grazed serenely on the lush carpet of green grass.

Around the next bend in the road, a sight that Dex would not soon forget appeared before him. A two-story sprawling ranch house stood against the breathtaking backdrop of majestic mountain ranges. A barn right off the pages of a New England calendar lay in the distance, as did other not-readily-identifiable structures. A corral he recognized from its circular design encompassed a large area near the barn. His gaze shifted back to the house. It was the house that held the place of honor among nature's and man's embellishments. With the authenticity of a perfect reproduction from the set of an old black-and-white Western movie, the house looked homey, inviting.

"Home sweet home," he murmured as his heart rate increased, sending adrenaline surging through his veins.

"Yessiree Bob," Leanne agreed.

She smiled, a gesture that sent a spear of heat straight through him. Were all the women out here so innocent-looking and apparently sweet?

"Come on, they'll be waiting."

She got out, skirted the hood and reached in back for his bag before he had the presence of mind to react.

Dex wrenched the door open and all but fell out of the truck. "I'll get that," he insisted, grappling for his equilibrium and at the same time reaching for the heavy duffel. She was certainly stronger than she looked.

"Gran fixed your favorite for supper," she told him with another of those wide, sincere smiles.

He nodded, but hoped to God he could bow out of dinner, er, supper. He wasn't ready to play Ty Cooper to a larger audience just yet. And he didn't have a clue what Ty's favorite meal was supposed to be. Surely the Coopers would understand that he was exhausted after his trip and required an early retirement this evening.

Dex followed Leanne up the steps to the wooden porch that spanned the front of the house. A low growl froze him in his tracks. His eyes widened when his gaze sought and found the source of the sound. A dog. A large, rather fierce-looking animal that appeared poised to lunge at him. Dex had no experience with dogs to call upon. Grandmother Montgomery had allergies. Pets had never been allowed in the Montgomery residence.

"Lady," Leanne scolded. "Why would you growl at Ty? Just because he took a trip without you?" she said in that child-like tone adults took when speaking affectionately to children or animals. "He's only been gone a week. Now you be a good girl. You know better than to misbehave." She scratched the big animal, which Dex now recognized as a golden retriever, behind the ears.

"You should recognize me, Lady," he put in when Leanne looked up at him as if she expected some sort of reaction. He certainly wasn't about to reach down and touch the animal.

Leanne gave Lady's head one final pat. The dog lumbered away, then dropped onto the porch as if too tired or disgusted to pursue the situation further.

"Looks like you're not the only one feeling out of sorts this evening."

Dex feigned a laugh. "Jet lag," he repeated.

Leanne stared at him for one long moment. "Yeah. Maybe I don't want to go to Chicago if flying is that tough on you." She opened the front door and entered the house as if she lived there.

No locked door. No knock first. Dex would have been appalled at the Coopers' lack of security measures had his heart not been pounding like a drum in his chest. He had to find a way out of this. He would never fool these people.

"We're here!" Leanne shouted as she wandered down the hall.

"Welcome home!"

Dex jerked to an abrupt stop in the middle of the hall. The duffel thunked to the hardwood floor. What looked like a dozen people, of varying sizes and ages, all beaming smiles, and heading for him, crowded into the entry hall. A big banner reading Welcome Home! draped from one wall to the other. One would think that Ty had been gone for months.

An older woman, her gray hair in a tight bun, her hazel eyes shining with emotion, threw her arms around him first. "It's good to have you back home, son."

His Grandmother Cooper.

Dex opened his mouth to speak but no words formed. He felt suddenly overwhelmed with unfamiliar emotions as those slim, frail arms tightened around him.

A strong hand clapped him on the back even before the older woman released him. "Take that hat off, young man."

Dex turned to greet the man who'd spoken. Tall, slim, thinning gray hair, brown eyes. Dex dragged the hat from his head and dropped it on a nearby table. "Pa," he offered, the single-syllable word steeped in too many emotions to sort. This was his mother's father.

The older man slung an arm around his shoulder and started down the hall, Dex in tow. "Come on, boy, supper's waiting.'' He paused and beamed a proud smile in Dex's direction. ''We're glad you're home, son.''

Everyone started talking at once then. Dex lost track of the number of times his journey was halted so that he could be hugged and welcomed home. His Grandmother Cooper insisted that Leanne stay for supper. For some reason he couldn't begin to understand, he was glad she agreed to stay. He'd analyze that bit of irony later.

Right now it took all his powers of concentration to watch his step. Especially since three small children all but clung to his legs as he followed the crowd into the dining room. He felt certain his back would be bruised considering all the hearty poundings he'd taken from the male Coopers. For these people, outward displays of affection were apparently a way of life.

The dining table was long, like the one in his home back in Atlanta, only this one was a rustic country style, the tabletop scarred from years of everyday use. The heavy stoneware dishes bore the same worn appearance and spoke of both hard times and good times, neither of which were forgotten or taken for granted.

The elder Coopers occupied the head positions at the table. Leanne sat across from Dex next to Angelica, the five-year-old daughter of Ty's adopted brother Chad. Chad and his wife also sat on that side. Next to Dex was Chad's older brother Court, his wife, and their four-year-old twin boys. At least he hoped he had the right name with the right brother.

Ty had explained that Court and Chad were the

sons of Grandmother Cooper's younger sister who had died years ago, leaving the boys alone in the world since their father had already passed away. The Coopers had gladly taken in the boys, adopting them and rearing them as Ty's brothers. Dex suddenly wanted to know what that sort of love was like. That kind of family bond. Though he knew his grandparents in Atlanta loved him, it wasn't the same.

"So, did you have a pleasant trip?" Grandmother Cooper asked as she offered a platter of steaks to Dex.

Dex stared at the enormous platter as he accepted it. Big, thick, juicy cuts of beef. He selected the smallest portion then passed the platter to Court. "It was…" How the hell was it? he wondered. "…as well as can be expected, I suppose," he said noncommittally.

Grandfather Cooper snorted. "I told you not to get your hopes up, son. You're just like your mother, always dreaming big dreams. But sometimes you just have to be satisfied with the way things are."

Dex stared at the older man. *Just like his mother.* His mother'd had big dreams? What kind of dreams? He suddenly wanted to know.

"Enough of that," Grandmother Cooper scolded when Dex was relatively sure his grandfather would have gone on. "Ty's just gotten home. He can tell us about the business part of his trip tomorrow."

She smiled at Dex and he had the abrupt, overwhelming feeling that it was exactly like seeing his mother smile. Before he could dwell further on the gesture a bowl of green beans was thrust under his chin. Dex peered down at the clearly overcooked vegetable. The whole meal was a ticket to an early grave.

Green beans, cooked with what appeared to be a hunk of meat consisting totally of fat, steak, potatoes brimming with golden butter, and a slab of cornbread that looked as though it could keep them all fed for a week. The kind of meal the Montgomerys avoided at all costs.

Not a single lettuce leaf was in sight.

Dex surveyed the large group gathered around the table. Hadn't any of them heard about eating healthy? Without warning, something hit him square in the chest. A green bean lay on the table, a greasy spot just above the fourth button soiled the tan-colored shirt he wore.

Across the wide expanse of worn, but well-polished oak Angelica smiled innocently at him. Dex peered at her in confusion for a moment, then at the bean once more. Had she thrown it at him? He lifted his gaze back to her just in time to see her use her spoon to launch another one in his direction. This one hit high on his right shoulder.

Dex frowned, uncertain of what course of action he should take, if any. He hadn't spent any time around children. He only knew that they were messy and cried a lot. This one appeared intent on the former. He scanned the other adult faces. All were engrossed in eating or some discussion about the ranch he probably wouldn't have understood even if he'd been listening.

Just when Angelica, an evil grin plastered across her pretty little face, prepared to fire at him once more, her father's hand closed over hers. "Stop that, young lady," he said firmly.

Relieved, Dex relaxed. "She's a pretty good shot, Court," he offered conversationally.

Everyone stopped talking and stared at him. What had he done? The sound of blood roaring through his ears made the silence deafening. Had he made a mistake already?

And then he knew.

"Chad," Dex amended, then shook his head. He'd called the man by the wrong name. Dex shrugged. "Jet lag," he offered in explanation.

All nodded, some even laughed and seemed to be satisfied with that excuse. All but Leanne, who studied him inquisitively. Flashing her a strained smile, Dex focused on the food on his plate. He'd have to be more careful. His head was throbbing, his heart pounding. But he was here now. He might as well give this trading places thing a shot. There was no reason he couldn't do it. He glanced at the child sitting across the table. She gave him one of those I'm-not-through-with-you-yet looks. Then again, maybe he couldn't do it.

Had he lost his mind entirely? Dex slowly studied the people seated around the table. Uncertainty undermined his newly found determination. How in the world was he supposed to fool all of them? When his gaze settled on his Grandmother Cooper again she chose that precise moment to turn toward him. Another of those heartwarming smiles spread across her lovely face. This was why he was here. *This* was his opportunity to learn what kind of person his mother had been. To see pictures…to learn about her past.

And maybe to somehow understand how a family as seemingly loving and generous as this one could take one child and turn their back on the other.

Chapter Two

Dex felt like a character from an episode of a reality TV show.

He was mentally and physically drained, but his first meal with the Coopers was nearing an end at last. The moment anyone seated around the large table made a move signaling the event was officially over, he intended to excuse himself for the evening. His senses were on overload. Too much conversation, too many different voices and personalities. He'd definitely taken for granted the experience of quiet dining. He doubted he would do that again anytime soon. This level of stimuli during a meal couldn't possibly bode well for the digestive system.

Not to mention he'd ingested more saturated fats in one sitting than he had in a lifetime of eating his usual cuisine. He had to admit, however, that the steak had been more than palatable...tasty even. If what he'd been served tonight was indicative of Cooper beef, then the quality was premium.

He could see now why Ty felt compelled to pursue larger markets. The product was certainly worth the extra effort.

"We'll clear, ladies," Chad, or at least Dex thought it was Chad, said as he pushed back his chair and stood.

At this point Dex wasn't sure of anything except that he had to be alone.

"Why, thank you, honey," Chad's wife—Jenny, if Dex remembered correctly—crooned with a wide smile.

Following the example of the other men, Dex stood as well. He knew a moment of panic as he considered what he should do next. He'd never had to clear a table before. How difficult could it be? Drawing on years of experience of eating at restaurants, he reached for his plate and glass like the waiters who'd served him in the past.

"No way, brother," Court said from beside him. "You've got the night off." Court winked. "Besides, you have company to see to."

Dex blinked, uncertain what the man meant. What company?

"Oh, don't be silly, Court," Leanne chided. She pushed to her feet. "I can see myself out. It's past time I got home." She leaned down and pressed a quick kiss to Grandmother Cooper's cheek. "Thank you for having me to supper."

"Anytime, dear," she returned. "Anytime. You tell your mama I said hello."

"I sure will." Leanne glanced at Dex. "Well, I guess I'll be going."

Court elbowed him. "I'll...ah...see you to the door," Dex offered, suddenly remembering his manners, and realizing, just as abruptly, that the rest of the family clearly considered Leanne his company.

Still trying to figure that one out, Dex followed her into the front hall. "Thank you again for picking me up at the airport," he offered for lack of anything else to say.

"I didn't mind," she said, turning back to him when she stopped at the door. "I hope something good comes of your trip, Ty. I do know how much it means to you."

The sincerity in her eyes was so genuine that it moved Dex. Or maybe it was just those big blue eyes that affected him. And all that silky blond hair. For the first time since he'd met Leanne, Dex took a moment to really look at her. She was of medium height, her figure curvy, voluptuous. Nothing like the waif-thin women he usually preferred. The well-worn jeans and button-up blouse were accessorized with scuffed boots and a leather belt that cinched her tiny waist. The smallness of her waist accentuated her womanly hips and particularly full breasts. Dex drew in a tight breath. She certainly had a nice set of...

"Are you sure you're all right, Ty?"

Her question jolted him to attention. He blinked and dragged his gaze back to hers. Though she looked concerned, he could well imagine what she must think at the moment. He'd blatantly stared at her breasts. Thoroughly measured her body with his eyes. He had no doubt he'd lost his mind. The chances of a speedy recovery looked dim at best.

"I'm fine...really," he insisted. "Fine."

She nodded, the doubt clear in her eyes. "Well, I'll see you around then."

He felt his head bob up and down though he

couldn't recall issuing the necessary command. "Sure," he managed to choke out.

She hesitated when she would have opened the door, adding a new layer of tension to his already unbearable state. "I almost forgot." She stared up at him. "Are we still on for the dance Friday night?"

Dance? Ty hadn't mentioned any dance. Worry tightened around his throat like a noose. "Dance?" he echoed his bewildered thought.

"The annual barbecue and dance to raise money for the volunteer fire department. You haven't forgotten, have you?"

Faced with her expression of disappointment and maybe even a little hurt he heard himself say, "No, no. I haven't forgotten. I'm just too tired to think, that's all." He shrugged. "Sure, we're still on," he added, using her words.

Her face brightened. The smile with which she gifted him shifted something in his chest. How could a mere smile have such a mesmerizing effect?

"Good night," she murmured.

"Good night." Despite everything, he just couldn't help himself. He felt his lips curl upward as he stared deeply into those wide, blue eyes.

Before he could fathom her intent, she tiptoed and placed a chaste kiss on his jaw then rushed out the door.

Dex stared after her as she hurried away. He didn't close the door until the tail lights of her truck had disappeared around the bend. He touched his jaw where she'd kissed him and he felt weak with something he couldn't name. What was it about this woman—this place—that made him feel so strange?

He couldn't recall ever having felt so flustered, so uncertain of who he was.

"Dex Montgomery," he murmured. "You're Dex Montgomery." He had to remember that.

"Ty."

Dex turned to find Grandmother Cooper waiting near the bottom of the stairs. He smiled automatically, which was not his custom. He couldn't say for sure whether he intended the gesture or if he'd simply done it so she would smile back at him. There was something about her smile.

"I know you're worn out, son," she said kindly. "Why don't you call it a night? You can tell us all about your trip in your own time." She winked covertly. "I left a present for you in your room."

Dex felt weightless as he watched her walk away. His grandmother had gotten him a gift. Why that should give him such pleasure, he had no clue. But it waited for him in his room.

Dex stilled. No. It was waiting for him in Ty's room.

Where the hell was Ty's room?

How COULD SHE have kissed him?

Leanne slammed on her brakes and skidded to a frustrated halt a few feet from her own front porch. She shut off the lights and engine and heaved a disgusted sigh.

She'd kissed Ty. At least it had been only on the cheek, but she'd kissed him nonetheless.

She had undoubtedly lost her everloving mind. Why else would she have behaved so irrationally?

Been so forward? There was no telling what he thought.

Depressed now more than disgusted, she laid her forehead against the steering wheel and considered how she would ever face him again.

Warmth spread through her as the brief meeting of her lips and his stubbled jaw played through her mind once more. Though always clean-shaven, Ty's dark features left him with a five o'clock shadow every evening. She'd always imagined that beneath that darkly handsome exterior beat the heart of a truly sinful lover. A man who could please a woman. The details of his muscular chest ran through her mind. Never had the idea of Ty's virility or masculinity intrigued her so.

Leanne straightened, frowning. She'd seen Ty shirtless hundreds of times. He was a strong, well-built man. She felt certain he would make some woman very happy some day. But not her. She loved him like a *brother*. Not once in her entire life had she felt even remotely sexually attracted to him.

Not once.

Until today.

The moment their gazes had locked at the airport she'd felt something…something different. She shook her head and climbed out of her old truck. The Coopers as well as her own mother had been trying to push the two of them together for as long as she could remember. She knew they meant well, wanted their children to be happy. But Leanne had other plans. She wanted to fall head over heels in love with a man who would sweep her off her feet. And she wanted to be financially independent.

"Yeah, right," she grumbled as she trudged up the steps to her house. Just how was she supposed to meet Mr. Right and be financially independent when she was barely keeping her head above water in more ways than one?

She unlocked the front door and went inside. Being careful not to make any more noise than necessary she closed and locked the door behind her. The stairs to the second floor proved a bit trickier when it came to her efforts to be soundless. But Leanne knew all the spots to avoid. She didn't want to wake her mother. Lord knew, sleep was the only peace she found.

Joanna Watley suffered with debilitating weakness and often a great deal of pain. Dr. Baker had done everything he could for her, to no avail. She needed further testing and a specialist or maybe even a team of specialists. But there was no money for such extravagances that would likely do no good, her mother insisted. Without medical insurance the burden of cost fell squarely on Leanne and her mother's shoulders. A burden Leanne was ready to accept if her mother would only allow it.

Leanne paused outside her mother's bedroom door. She slept soundly. Leanne eased into the room and sat down on the edge of the bed to watch her sleep. She was a truly beautiful woman. Long blond hair, peppered with a little gray, and blue eyes. The same blue eyes Leanne had inherited. Leanne's father used to say that she and her mother looked more like sisters than mother and daughter. He'd always known how to bring a smile to her mother's lips. It just didn't seem fair that he'd died four years ago, and then last

year her mother's debilitating illness had struck.
Leanne blinked back her tears. She loved her mother
dearly and she would do whatever she could to help
her.

Joanna Watley had a stubborn streak a mile wide,
though. Leanne had begged her to sell the ranch and
use the money for whatever medical treatment she
needed. Joanna refused. She insisted that they hang
on to the ranch no matter what. She'd be all right in
time, she always said.

But that time never came. She only got worse.
Leanne felt a burst of desperation in her chest. How
would she ever convince her mother to listen to her?
She probably couldn't, which left Leanne with only
one choice. She had to make the money herself. She
couldn't leave her mother alone all day to get a job
in town. And anyway, Leanne had no real skills. With
her father's ill health, then his death, and now her
mother's illness, she'd been taking care of the ranch
since she'd graduated high school. There'd been no
time or money for college.

Instead, she spent every spare moment attempting
to complete what her father had begun—turning their
ranch into a dude ranch. Dude ranches were wildly
popular, and this area of Montana was particularly
attractive to tourists. No one else in the vicinity had
one. It would be a gold mine, if only Leanne could
finish the job.

The guest cabins had been constructed. The pool
was pretty much complete. If Leanne worked hard
enough, saved every cent possible, she could get it up
and running. With the dozen horses they had kept and
the guest cabins and pool ready, she could prepare to

open this fall. She might not make much in the beginning, but her reputation would build. Then she would have the money to send her mother wherever she needed to go without selling the ranch.

But that seemed a lifetime away. Though Dr. Baker didn't feel her mother's symptoms were life-threatening, it was definitely debilitating, leaving her with a miserable existence.

Leanne blinked back a fresh wave of tears. She didn't want her mother to suffer like this. But she was an adult, Leanne couldn't make her go to a specialist.

"You home already?"

Leanne produced a smile at the weak sound of her mother's voice. "I didn't mean to wake you."

"I'm glad you came in to say goodnight." Her mother frowned. "But you shouldn't have hurried home."

"I didn't want to stay out too late. You feeling all right?"

Her mother dredged up a smile from a source of strength Leanne could only imagine possessing. "I'm just fine. How did Ty's trip go?"

"He won't know for a while." Leanne looked away. She didn't want to get into a discussion of Ty with her mother. Not tonight.

"Is something wrong, Leanne?"

Her mother read her too well. "Oh no," she assured her. "Everything's fine." But it wasn't, she thought, remembering the way he'd looked at her in the truck on the way home and then at the door when they'd said goodnight. Something was definitely different.

Her mama's hand closed over hers. "I wish I could

make you see, child, what a good husband Ty would make. I don't know why you don't trust your mama's instincts.''

Here they went again. Leanne sighed. ''I know he'd make a fine husband, Mama, that's not the problem.''

Joanna shook her head. ''You've read too many of those paperbacks. You keep expecting some knight in shining armor to come take you away. Well, that ain't the way it works. You know Ty and his family. They're good folks. Marrying Ty is the right thing to do.'' She squeezed her daughter's hand. ''It's the only way you'll ever save this ranch.''

There it was, the bottom line. The weight of saving the family ranch fell squarely on Leanne's shoulders. ''I know all that,'' she said. ''It's just that I don't feel that way toward Ty.'' At least she hadn't until today. Maybe that was just a fluke.

Her mother sighed wearily. ''You'll see, Leanne. Everything will be fine. You'll learn to love Ty that way. He's a good man. It's what we all want.''

Leanne arched a skeptical brow. ''You might be counting your chickens before they hatch considering he hasn't asked yet. Maybe he won't.''

Joanna smiled. ''Oh, he will. The Coopers have wanted to combine this land with their own for two generations.'' Her mother patted her hand. ''He'll ask. It's just a matter of time.''

Opting not to argue the issue further, Leanne kissed her mother's forehead. ''Goodnight, Mama.''

Leanne left her mother's room and headed toward her own. According to what her mother had told her eons ago, the Coopers had been disappointed when their only daughter, Tara, hadn't married the only Watley son, Leanne's father. Instead, she'd married the son of the Cooper family's archrivals, a Montgomery. Tara and her husband had died in a tragic accident just one year later, leaving their infant sons, one of which had died shortly thereafter.

Now, the sole Cooper heir and the Watley heiress were once more being groomed for merging the two properties.

But that wasn't the kind of merger Leanne was looking for.

After dragging off her boots, she stripped off her clothes and slipped into a warm flannel gown. It was May, not quite summer yet, and nights were still a bit chilly. She crawled beneath the covers and tried without success to block Ty Cooper's image from her mind.

Being Ty's wife wouldn't be such a chore, she admitted. He was handsome, broad-shouldered and a gentleman in the truest sense of the word. She remembered well her first day in kindergarten. The school bully had made fun of her on the playground. Ty had come to her rescue. Though nine years her senior, he seemed always to be there, taking care of her.

She heaved a weary breath and flopped over on her side. But she didn't love him, and she doubted he loved her. The Coopers already leased part of her grazing land. In fact, that lease money was all that stood between the Watleys and the poorhouse. Two or three times in the last year, they'd skated far too close to foreclosure for comfort.

No matter, Leanne didn't want to get married because it made financial sense. The lease appeared to be working for both families without a marriage to seal the deal. Why didn't they just leave it at that? Even if she somehow managed to bring life to her father's dream, it wouldn't prevent the Coopers from continuing to run cattle on her land. On the contrary, the cattle would add Western ambiance to her dude ranch. But her mother wouldn't hear of it. She intended Leanne to marry Ty.

Maybe Leanne could work up the nerve to talk it over with Ty. She couldn't imagine that he liked this matchmaking business any better than she did. Surely he would see reason. Then they would both be free to look for their own true loves.

That warm sensation that had bloomed in her middle when she'd kissed Ty suddenly swirled inside her once more. She remembered the searing heat in his eyes when he'd looked at her, as if for the first time, before she'd said goodnight. She shook her head and hugged her pillow. It was ridiculous. He wouldn't be able to make her feel that way again. She was sure of it.

Spending time with him at the dance on Friday night would prove it.

The dance.

Leanne sat straight up. She had absolutely nothing to wear to the dance.

She mentally ticked off every dress in her closet. It didn't take long, she only owned three. She couldn't wear any of those old flour sacks. She chewed her lower lip. But she sure hated to spend the money to buy something new. Though she supposed that it was time she bought a new church dress. The whole congregation was likely tired of looking at the same old three over and over.

Funny, she mused with growing self-deprecation, she hadn't worried about anything new to wear to the dance until tonight. What was it about Ty this evening that made her suddenly feel so strangely attracted to him? What made this day any different from the thousands of others they'd shared in the past twenty years?

Leanne dropped back onto her pillows. She couldn't answer that question. She would just have to wait and see if that zing of desire happened again.

Probably not, she decided. Lightning never struck the same place twice.

Did it?

DEX HAD FOUND Ty's room with only a couple of false starts. Fortunately no one had been around to see those blunders. The whole Cooper clan had gathered in the family room to watch television after he'd excused himself.

Dex felt immensely grateful for the reprieve. His feet were relieved as well. He simply couldn't imagine what made cowboys believe that boots were comfortable. Apparently their feet had been molded for the footwear since birth.

How would he endure the ill-fitting get-up he was supposed to wear for the duration of this ruse? He wondered then how Ty was faring in Atlanta. The notion that Grandfather Montgomery was probably completely fooled pleased Dex entirely too much. He knew he should feel some regret, but he didn't. Not in the proper sense anyway. He regretted wearing the boots. He didn't look forward to pretending to be someone he wasn't. Yet, he savored the idea of the discoveries he would make. He would learn about his mother and the people who'd turned their backs on him as a mere infant.

And he intended to teach the Montgomerys a little lesson as well. He and Ty were the victims here. No one could call any part of this entire sham fair. Their whole lives were based on one huge, bogus negotiation strategy.

Was Ty lying in Dex's bed in Atlanta and wondering how the Montgomerys could have chosen Dex over him?

It wasn't a good feeling. Dex knew first-hand.

He thought of his Grandmother Cooper and the way her smile did strange things to his heart. He glanced at the unopened gift waiting on the bureau. A part of him wanted desperately to open it, but it wasn't really for him. It was for Ty. Dex looked away. It was all for Ty. Even the smiles that made Dex feel as if he was looking into an expression his mother would have freely offered.

The bottom line was, he wanted to know more...to somehow understand. Besides, the elder Coopers intrigued him. He wanted to know what made them tick. What had precipitated the choices they'd made all those years ago? And before he returned to Atlanta, Dex would have the answers. He was very good at getting to the bottom of things.

Surviving in the shark-infested waters of HMOs and high finance had taught him a good many things. Not the least of which was survival of the fittest.

But nothing he'd ever learned or experienced had

prepared him for the attraction brewing between Leanne Watley and him. Dex mentally reviewed every moment of the time they'd spent together. He decided it was her innocence, her naïveté that drew him. He'd never known a woman quite like her. She also intrigued him. Ty had likened her to a sister. But the vibes Dex had gotten from her were in no way sisterly.

He scowled as he considered the dance he was supposed to escort her to on Friday night. Had he imagined it or had she seemed excited at the prospect? Then again, it could have been him who was excited.

Dex closed his eyes and banished thoughts of Leanne.

He was a stranger in a strange place. He didn't know what he was feeling. If there was something between Leanne and Ty, Dex had no place in it. He'd have to ask Ty about her when they spoke. And he'd have to find a way to avoid her for the next few days. The last thing he needed was a case of lust for his brother's woman.

Brother. The word still felt alien, but it was an undeniable fact. He had a brother. He had another family. The question was, what on earth would he do with them when he had the answers he wanted?

Better yet, what would the Coopers do when they discovered he'd pulled the wool over their eyes?

He pounded his pillow with a fist and tried to get comfortable. Getting comfortable was as impossible as finding any kind of resolution to this quandary.

It was a lose-lose situation.

There would be no winner when he and Ty revealed their true identities and returned to their respective homes.

Maybe trading places hadn't been such a clever idea after all.

Chapter Three

It wasn't a dream.

Dex sat up in bed just as the rising sun spilled its warm glow across the aged hardwood floor. Morning had arrived with a good deal more pomp and circumstance than Dex was accustomed to. The crowing of a rooster and the clanging of pots were sounds he could have gone the rest of his life without hearing at the crack of dawn.

His valet George always greeted him promptly at 6:00 a.m. with a tray of steaming coffee and an array of newspapers. The day's wardrobe awaited him in the dressing room when he completed his morning workout and shower. By 9:00 a.m. he was at the office ready to work.

But not today.

Sometime during the night as he tossed and turned he had made his decision. He would consider this a mini-vacation at a rather rustic resort. There was no reason not to relax and enjoy. He would have a much-needed, whether he chose to admit the need or not, break from the pressure of running a major medical corporation, and he would learn about the Coopers.

When he and Ty were ready they would go public. But not yet.

Dex threw the covers back and climbed out of bed. The wood floor felt cool beneath his feet, a definite contrast to the plush carpeting of his own bedroom. He strode over to a large armoire, which he had ascertained last night was in lieu of a closet. Scowling, he rifled through it. The shirts were all alike in design, the colors varied slightly.

Disgusted by the lack of selection, he dragged a shirt from its hanger and went to the bureau in search of pants. He found several pairs of scruffy-looking jeans and selected the least offensive pair. In another drawer he found white tube socks. For the boots, he supposed with a grimace.

From the duffel bag he retrieved a pair of his own underwear. He drew the line at wearing another man's shorts.

Since he found no robe, he tugged on the jeans and slipped into the hall, scanning warily for any of the Cooper clan. Silence ruled on the second floor. Everyone appeared to have gone downstairs already.

Good.

Dex padded down the hall to the communal bathroom. Though large and well stocked with linens and bath accessories, it was singular nonetheless. He lowered the toilet lid and placed his attire for the day there. He tried locking the door but, after several frustrated failures, gave up. The latch wouldn't work. Everyone was downstairs anyway, why sweat it? He grabbed a towel from the linen closet and slung it over the shower curtain rod. After peeling off the jeans, he adjusted the water to an inviting temperature and then stepped beneath the hot spray.

His eyes closed in appreciation. Dex relaxed for the first time since this adventure had begun.

Despite his best intentions not to think about her again, the image of Leanne Watley filled his mind. Those big blue eyes and that silky blond hair. His gut clenched at the thought of threading his fingers in those lovely tresses. The feel of her lips against his jaw sent a stab of desire straight to his loins. His body reacted instantly and his mind conjured up Leanne's even more enticing assets.

He wasn't supposed to be thinking about her that way. Forcing his eyes open, he banished the image. If anything, she was Ty's girlfriend. He wasn't Ty. He couldn't allow this *thing* to progress.

"Fool," he muttered.

Dex grabbed the bar of soap and began soaping his body. He didn't need any complications during his stay here. He had to keep this simple.

For all parties concerned.

Rinsing his well-lathered body he frowned when his gaze halted at his feet. He cocked his head away from the spray and stared at the water swirling around his feet and then down the drain. He looked at the soap in his hand, it was blue. Then why was the water going down the drain tinted green?

An explosion of giggles launched him into action. Dex jerked the shower curtain open. Court's sons, the four-year-old twins, stood next to the tub, an empty mouthwash bottle in their hands.

"What are you doing?" Dex demanded.

The two dark-haired boys looked first at each other,

then at Dex. They dropped the plastic container and ran for their lives in a flash of Scooby-Doo pajamas, leaving the door wide open and shouting, "Mornin', Uncle Ty!"

Swearing under his breath, Dex stamped over to the door, leaving a trail of water on the tile floor, and slammed it shut. He whipped back around and almost fell in his haste. Catching himself, he retraced, much more slowly this time, his path. As soon as he'd washed his hair and rinsed the soap from his skin, he dried himself and the floor.

He thought about the bean-throwing incident and then the mouthwash. Didn't anyone discipline these children?

As a child he was never allowed to behave in such a manner. His grandparents had ensured his proper training from the age of four. Though he'd never had a nanny, at least not that he could recall. He remembered clearly the first day George, his valet, began his employment as Dex's teacher and mentor to the finer points of etiquette.

Dex stared at his reflection in the mirror and wondered what George would think of him now. Pretending to be someone else and wearing this getup. Give him Armani any day. George would likely shake his regal head and make that annoying tsking sound. Since he wasn't here, Dex didn't have to worry about that.

Back in Ty's room, Dex tugged on the cursed boots. His feet ached even before he stood. The gift on the bureau snagged his attention again.

Would it be perceived as odd if he didn't open the present right away? Would his seeming indifference to the act of generosity hurt his grandmother's feelings? He sighed. He had no choice but to open it.

Dex placed his hands on either side of the box and hesitated still. His heart thundered in his chest. This was ridiculous. It was just a present. It wasn't even for him. Not really. The gesture meant nothing to him personally. He removed the lid, the scent of leather filling his nostrils, and studied the gift beneath. Leather chaps. The perfect gift for a cowboy, he supposed ruefully. He picked up the note from inside the box and read it.

Ty, I knew you needed a new set of chaps but wouldn't buy any for yourself. Your old ones out in the tack room are being recycled. A welcome-home present seemed like a good enough reason to buy new ones for you.

Love, Gran.

Dex closed his eyes and struggled with the emotions suddenly churning inside him. The Montgomerys never did little things like this for each other. He stared at the note once more. He couldn't even remember the last time he'd received a personal note from his grandparents. If either of them wanted to tell him anything they sent a message with a member of the household staff or his personal secretary. They didn't bother with personal notes.

But then, the Montgomerys had other assets. Just because he was angry with them at the moment didn't mean he failed to recognize how much they loved him. Gifts such as this were never necessary. Dex always had everything he wanted given to him well before he needed it.

The Coopers had nothing on the Montgomerys on that score. Of course, he wasn't actually keeping score. Was he?

Twenty minutes and a half dozen false starts later, Dex made his grand entrance into the dining room. Donning the chaps hadn't been easy, but he was fully garbed now. From the hat to the boots.

"Good morning," he said cheerily to the rest of the group assembled around the table.

Grandfather Cooper choked on his coffee. Grandmother Cooper's eyes widened in a look of disbelief. The rest of the family burst into laughter. Dex frowned. What was so funny? He looked down at himself and then back at them. He looked exactly like the cowboys he'd seen in the movies.

What was the problem?

Maybe they'd all heard about the mouthwash episode. He narrowed his gaze in the direction of the twins.

"Planning on roping and branding cattle this morning, bro?" Chad suggested, barely restraining a new wave of laughter.

Dex didn't get the joke.

"Sorry to be the one to tell you," Court added between chuckles. "But today we're cleaning out the barn and surveying the pastures. You won't need your chaps today."

He was *over*dressed, he realized then. He opened his mouth to explain, but then thought better of it. What could he say? That he was ignorant to the ways of cowboys?

Grandmother Cooper gestured to the vacant chair next to her. "Take your hat off, son, and have a seat. Your breakfast is getting cold."

Before taking his seat, Dex, determined to save face, leaned down and kissed his grandmother's lilac-scented cheek. "Thank you for the chaps, Gran. I wanted you to get the full effect," he told her as if he'd known exactly what he was doing when he put them on.

Court and Chad still looked amused. Grandfather Cooper had regained his composure with only a hint of a smile lingering about his expression.

Grandmother Cooper smiled kindly. "Well, you accomplished your mission, son." She patted his hand. "You look very handsome."

The telephone rang before Dex had a chance to sit down.

"Ty, would you get that since you're still up?" Grandfather Cooper asked.

"Then we can get the *going* effect as well," Chad teased, sending the younger Coopers into another fit of laughter.

Dex clenched his jaw long enough to restrain his temper. "Be happy to oblige," he drawled, doing his best imitation of John Wayne.

He straightened slowly, allowing the phone to ring once more in order to give him the general direction in which to look. The hall. He sauntered from the room, knowing full well Court and Chad were grinning behind his back. Judging by the way they were dressed, he definitely looked like the circus clown leaving center ring.

Annoyed more with himself than anyone else, he scooped up the receiver and barked a hello.

"Dex?"

"Ty?"

"Yeah, it's me."

Thank God.

Dex stretched the cord and got as far away from the dining-room door as possible. "Why the hell didn't you tell me about the investors and the chaps? And Leanne," he muttered hotly.

"Me? Why didn't you tell me about that piranha you've got working for you! And I think George is suspicious."

"What?" Dex was confused. What piranha?

"Bridget whatever-her-name-is," Ty snapped. "She won't leave me alone."

"Oh." Dex stroked his chin thoughtfully. Bridget could be relentless and territorial. Their physical relationship had always been convenient, nothing else. Not that she hadn't tried to make it more. "Tell her you want the monthly status reports early. That should keep her busy for a while. My best advice would be to avoid her if you can."

"What about George?" Ty demanded. "How do I handle him?"

"Tell him you're not in the mood to talk if he starts prying. That usually does the trick." It sounded as if Ty had the same problems Dex did. "What about your investment meeting?" he prodded.

"There's nothing to tell," Ty related what Dex already knew. "I'm trying to expand the Circle C's market and improve profit."

"I thought as much."

"You'll get an official response in a few days," Ty went on. "Let me know the moment you receive it. I'm anxious to know which way the wind is going to blow on my proposal."

Dex cocked an eyebrow. "All right. And you let me know how it goes there."

"Will do. Anything else? I don't know how much longer I can hide in this bathroom. George may be spying on me as we speak."

Dex chuckled. Yes, Ty was feeling the pressure too. "One more thing. About Leanne."

"What about her?"

"I thought you told me you were just friends."

"We are," Ty said flatly. "I guess I forgot to mention that our families would like it otherwise."

"I guess you did," Dex retorted dryly. "And this dance?"

"The one on Friday night? It's just a fund-raiser. I take Leanne every year just to keep the peace between the two families. A little bit of square dancing, foot stomping."

To keep the peace? Dex didn't even want to know what that meant. "Okay, I guess I can take her."

"You'd better be nice to Leanne and behave around her," Ty warned. "She's young and innocent and I don't want her hurt in all this."

"Neither do I," Dex said, surprised that his brother felt it necessary to warn him.

"Good. Now, how's my family?"

Dex heard the wistfulness in his voice. Ty missed his family. Could Dex say the same? Maybe, he wasn't sure…yet. "The Coopers are fine. I have to go. They're waiting for me."

When Ty didn't respond, Dex added, "Ty, I have to go."

"Okay, but one more thing. What's between you and this Dr. Stovall?"

"Dr. Stovall?" Dex paused, searching his brain for recognition. "Nothing. She's a pediatrician, I believe, at the hospital. Sort of a do-gooder—"

"There's nothing wrong with that," Ty interjected sharply.

Dex sighed. This did not sound good. "Listen, Ty, watch your step. I have to come back there, remember?"

"Don't worry. Everything's under control."

"Good. I'll talk to you when I can. Gotta go."

Dex hung up the receiver. It took him three long beats to prepare himself to reenter the dining room.

"It was one of the people I met in Chicago," he announced to the expectant faces still gathered around the table. "I should have word in a few days."

Nods and sounds of acknowledgment echoed around the room. Grandfather Cooper maintained a solemn, clearly skeptical expression.

Dex pulled his chair out and sat down. He looked at his plate, laden with eggs, bacon and biscuits, just in time to see a Cheerio land in the middle of the two sunny-side up eggs. His gaze met the wicked one belonging to his five-year-old niece, who was sitting on the opposite side of the table eating dry cereal from a bowl.

"Morning, Uncle Ty. You're a sleepyhead this mornin'," she accused.

Before Dex could think of an appropriate response, the rest of the men stood.

"The day's a wastin'. We'd better get going," Court suggested.

Another Cheerio plopped into Dex's plate. "I'll just eat something later," he said as he pushed up from his chair.

Grandmother Cooper frowned. "Don't rush out without your breakfast. You can catch up with your brothers later."

"Really," Dex assured her. "I'm good."

He left the room amid a chorus of "Uncle Tys!" resounding behind him. The twins had joined his niece, whom Dex now mentally dubbed the princess, in her farewell dramatics. Dex was pretty sure he'd never faced an opponent in the boardroom as formidable as those three kids.

Considering he was staying for the next few days under the same roof with them, he couldn't see how things could get any worse.

Once in the yard, Court said, "Chad, you want to oversee the barn work while Ty and I check out the fencing?"

"Will do."

Check out the fencing? He could do that, Dex decided. He followed Court to the barn. He paused in front of two stalls where a couple of massive horses resided.

"Saddle up, bro." Court clapped Dex on the back. "We've got a long day ahead of us."

Dex stared at the horse eyeing him suspiciously. Things had just gotten worse.

WHEN COURT finally called it a day, Dex had a complete understanding of the phrase "too long in the saddle." Every part of his lower body ached.

Sliding off the horse proved almost as difficult as mounting the huge beast had. By the time Dex had gotten into the saddle, Court was convinced the whole routine was an act to make him laugh. He'd laughed so hard he'd nearly cried when he'd had to tighten the cinch. Dex had tried to emulate Court as he saddled his own horse, but obviously he hadn't gotten it exactly right.

Taking small careful steps now, Dex headed toward the house. He needed a long, hot soak in the tub. He needed food and drink. No. Strike that. What he really needed was a half dozen or so protein shakes and then a double Scotch to finish it off.

He winced with each step. How could anyone like this lifestyle?

"Ty!"

Dex looked in the direction of the driveway and the unexpected but welcome sound of Leanne's voice. Already he knew it by heart. He was far too exhausted to consider why.

"Leanne," he acknowledged. "How are you today?"

She frowned, the gesture deepening the worry already clouding her expression. "We need to talk."

Something was wrong. Dex could see it in her eyes. He had the sudden urge to put his arm around her slender shoulders and assure her that everything would be fine. He gave himself a mental shake. Slow down, he warned. This was a mistake he did not intend to make. He recalled Ty's warning, but the urge to reassure her still nagged at him.

"Okay," he said instead, tucking his hands into his back pockets as a precaution.

She glanced around. "Not here." Her too-serious gaze landed on his once more. "Do you mind taking a ride to my place?"

The thought of sitting down in anything other than hot water almost made him say no, but the need to put that smile back on her pretty face prevailed.

"Why not?" He offered his arm. "I'd be pleased to."

Looking even more worried, she placed her arm in his and walked with him to her old truck. He opened the door for her then hustled around to the passenger door as quickly as he dared. But lowering himself into the seat proved the most difficult task.

"Are you sure you're feeling all right, Ty?" she asked, her fingers poised on the key in the ignition.

"Fabulous," Dex returned. "Just fabulous."

Shaking her head she started the engine.

This young lady seemed to know Ty better than anyone else. At least, she appeared to be the only one suspicious of Dex. He studied her lovely profile as she drove away from the Circle C. His muscles tightened just looking at her, in spite of his numerous aches.

He definitely had to watch his step around her.

LEANNE STOOD NEXT to Ty on her back porch and surveyed the dream her father had started five years ago. Her mother was resting in her room. She wouldn't like it if she knew what Leanne was about to do. But she had to tell him before she lost her nerve. She had to be honest, especially in light of recent events. She'd thought about it all night.

"I know you remember my father dreamed of turning this place into a dude ranch." She looked up at Ty. He looked at a loss for a moment, then nodded. Leanne peered back out over the nearly finished guest cabins and the waiting pool. "I want to make it happen, Ty," she said quietly, bracing herself for his response.

A full minute ticked by in silence.

"It's not what either of our families wants," she hastened to add. "I know that. But it wouldn't affect the grazing land. The Circle C could continue to lease the grazing land, all of it if they want. That wouldn't be a problem."

He looked at her then. She couldn't read what he was thinking or feeling. *Please,* she prayed, *let him understand.*

"This is what you want?" he asked, his tone carefully measured.

She nodded. "Very much."

He took off his hat and threaded his fingers through his hair, then replaced the hat as if he weren't used to having to bother. Her frown deepened. What was it that made him seem so different since he'd come back from Chicago? Even the way he talked was wrong somehow.

He took the four steps down from the porch then turned back to her. "Do you mind if we walk?"

She shook her head and hurried down the steps after him.

"Is the wiring and plumbing for the guest cottages complete?" he asked as they crossed the yard.

"Yes," she answered, afraid to hope. "I still have some painting and clean-up work to do. I'll have to buy furniture and pool chemicals. But I can be ready in a few months if I work on it every chance I get."

He paused near the pool and stared at her. "You're doing this alone?"

She sighed. "I didn't want to tell you." She hung her head. "I know what our families have always wanted." As difficult as it was, she met his gaze. "But *this* is what I want." How did she tell the man that she didn't want to spend the rest of her life as just his wife? She didn't want to hurt him. She cared about him. Deeply. She just wasn't in love with him. And she desperately wanted to see her father's wish come true.

"You could hire a contractor to finish up," he suggested, while studying the dark, mossy-green color of the pool water. It would take lots of chemicals to clear up that mess.

"That takes more money than I can afford to spend," she told him. It annoyed her because he of all people should know her circumstances. Well, at least, to a degree. She and her mother were too proud to tell the whole story. "I'd rather do the work myself anyway. That's what my father would have done."

He nodded. "Well, I think it's a great idea. Dude ranches are usually a big hit when operated properly. Are there—" He cut himself off abruptly. "Have you researched the probability of success?"

"If you're asking if I've done my homework, the answer is yes. There isn't one anywhere near here," she said, hardly believing he'd even asked. "Tourists love this part of the state, as you well know. I think it would be a tremendous success."

"All right, then." He braced his hands on his lean hips and studied the guest cabins that circled the pool. "I'll help you."

Leanne felt a ripple of shock. "What did you say?"

He shrugged awkwardly. "I'll help you. Court and Chad have things at the Circle C under control. There's no reason I can't pitch in here." His gaze locked with hers, and heat roared straight through her. "Isn't it the neighborly thing to do?"

Leanne couldn't argue with that reasoning.

Truth be told, she didn't want to. Another little shock wave shook her.

"Well, then." He smiled, sending her heart into a wild tattoo. "Let's do it."

Before she could stop herself she'd thrown her arms around him. "Thank you for understanding, Ty," she murmured against his neck.

"It's nothing," he argued, his posture rigid.

Darn it. She didn't want to cry. But the tears came anyway. She held onto him with all her might and cried into his shirt. "I'm sorry," she muttered.

"It's all right." His arms closed around her waist sending a new shard of heat slicing through her. "I—" He let go a heavy breath. His arms tightened around her, drawing her nearer. "It's okay," he said softly, his breath whispering against her cheek.

And she knew it would be.

Because Ty had told her so. He'd never let her down before.

Chapter Four

For a long time after Leanne dropped Dex back at the Cooper ranch he just stood watching as the dust that had billowed from beneath her old truck settled. He thought about the day he'd spent on horseback with Court, touring the grazing pastures, surveying the fencing. The Cooper ranch was pretty spectacular. Dex couldn't recall spending that much time in such a wide-open space ever before. He couldn't think about that without remembering the ribbing he'd taken from Chad when it took him three tries to mount Ty's horse. None of it seemed quite real.

Outside the Cooper family and Leanne, he'd been introduced to two Circle C ranch hands, a neighbor searching for a missing bull, and the local veterinarian making a house call. Everyone had the same easy-going, laid-back way about them. No one was in a hurry. Dex hadn't read the first hint of deception or ruthlessness in a single individual he'd met. It was completely unbelievable. And everyone helped everyone else. He and Court had spent an extra hour on horseback helping the neighbor look for his Brahman.

Dex, however, had balked at helping deliver a calf.

He'd stood back and allowed Court and the vet to handle that one.

He turned toward the house and studied the massive structure as the sun set behind it. With the purple and gold hues fading around it, the house and its serene setting looked picturesque and inviting. Like the home, the people here were friendly and caring.

Lines of confusion furrowed across his brow. How had these people, the salt of the earth, pretended for over thirty long years that he didn't even exist?

Dex shook his head. He might never know without staging an outright confrontation and demanding the answer. And right now he was too tired and sore for battle. He strode slowly to the house, up the steps and across the porch. He'd never been so glad to see a day end. As he reached for the door, a low growl stopped him.

A few feet away Lady stood very still, watching him with wary eyes and emitting a long fierce rumble.

"Behave, Lady," he commanded, recalling Leanne's words and trying his level best to sound confident. He told himself that he wasn't actually afraid, just cautious. But the sweat that broke out across his upper lip betrayed him.

The standoff lasted about ten seconds, but it felt like an eternity. Finally Lady sauntered over to what he'd come to think of as her favorite spot and lay down. She glared at him one last time as if she was still undecided as to whether he was worth any real effort.

Dex heaved a sigh of relief when she lowered her head to her front paws and closed her eyes. He'd made it past that barrier, he mused as he entered the house. Now if he could just make it up the stairs and to his room without being spotted, he'd be a happy man. He wanted a long, hot bath and a night of peace and quiet—alone. He had to think. To sort out all these confusing emotions.

The sound of feminine voices drifted to him from beyond the dining room. The women were likely preparing dinner, the men were probably still outside. The throaty laughter of his Grandmother Cooper stalled him at the bottom of the stairs. She sounded far younger than her years. He wondered if his mother had laughed like that, freely and with such heart.

Why did knowing more about his mother suddenly seem so important? He'd never suffered more than a fleeting moment of interest in the past. He had to remember what he'd come here for. To teach the Montgomerys a lesson and to show the Coopers what they'd missed all these years by turning their backs on him.

His jaw tightened. How had they chosen Ty over him? That was the million-dollar question. Had they simply flipped a coin? Who had made the first choice, a Cooper or a Montgomery? Was he taken only because the other child had already been selected?

Dex squared his shoulders and reminded himself he was Dex Montgomery, not Ty Cooper. This was not his home. These people weren't his family. Leanne was not his concern. Though he was sympathetic to her plight and had every intention of helping her while he was here, that was the extent of his plans where Leanne was concerned. The fact of the matter was, helping her would be to his benefit. It would get him away from the Coopers, the horses and that suspicious dog. Time away from the ranch would aid in retaining his cover. That was his only real motivation for offering her his assistance. In a couple of weeks this whole charade would be over and he'd be back in his own world.

Back where he belonged.

"Uncle Ty! Uncle Ty!"

Startled, Dex stared down at little Angelica tugging on his hand. "What is it?" he asked, more harshly than he'd intended. He wasn't accustomed to being accosted by little people.

"Hurry! Hurry!" she urged, pulling on his hand. "You have to come quick."

Reluctant, but uncertain what else to do, Dex allowed her to drag him along. "Where are we going?" he demanded.

"In here." She pointed to the family room. "The babies are causin' trouble."

A frown drew his eyebrows together as he attempted to decipher her panicked expression. "Trouble? What kind of trouble?"

"See." She paused in the open doorway of the family room and pointed. "If they fall, they gonna go *splat*," she said, her eyes huge.

Dex followed her gesture and did a double take. The boys were, rather successfully, climbing a floor-to-ceiling bookcase. Books fluttered to the floor like injured birds in their wake.

What should he do? If he shouted for help or for them to stop they might be startled and fall. His heart rate accelerated, making his chest tight. He had to rescue them before they hurt themselves. They were too young to realize the danger they were in, that much he knew.

Careful to be as quiet as possible, he rushed across the room, forgetting all about his numerous aches and pains, and grabbed the two boys, one in each arm, before they were even aware he was in the room. They squealed with what sounded like delight as he wagged them over to the sofa and plopped the two wriggling children down onto it. He stood there, glaring down at them, wondering how such small creatures could get into so much trouble.

"Do it again! Do it again!" they shouted in unison, bouncing on the overstuffed cushions like kangaroos.

Dex released the breath he'd been holding. Were kids always this much trouble? "Forget it," he told them when their chanting continued. He drew in another deep breath and let it out slowly to calm his racing heart.

"A story!" one countered. He couldn't say for sure if it was Danny or David. The two were identical.

"A story?" Only then did Dex notice the book one of the little devils held. "What about a story?" he grouched.

"Read it!" the two cried.

Dex harrumphed. "I don't think so."

"But, Uncle Ty, you always read us stories," Angelica chimed in, sidling up next to him. "Ever'day, almost."

Another thing Ty forgot to mention, Dex steamed. "Maybe later," he suggested in hopes of getting himself off the hook. He didn't do stories.

Angelica pouted. "Later we'll be in bed."

Later he'd be in bed, too. Three sets of eyes peered

up at him, expressions hopeful, almost pleading. One twin's lips quivered as if he might burst into tears. Oh no. If they all started to cry at once—

"Fine." He reached for the book. "One story and that's it."

His announcement was punctuated with exuberant cheers. The twins parted like the Red Sea, making space for him to sit on the sofa between them. The instant Dex sat down Angelica climbed onto his lap. A brief scuffle and heated debate ensued as the twins fought for their own section of territory. The three-some glared at each other when they were at last settled.

"Are we ready now?" Dex looked at Angelica and then at each of the boys.

All heads nodded.

Dex opened the book and read about Alice in Wonderland. The long version, apparently. By the time he finished, the twins and their tattling cousin were asleep.

Two little heads were snuggled against his chest, a third rested in the crook of his arm. He couldn't possibly move without waking one or all. Besides, he was totally exhausted. He needed to sleep himself. He'd tossed and turned most of last night. Tonight wasn't shaping up to be any better. One of the children sighed, and the sound was trusting, innocent and somehow mesmerizing to him.

He studied their little faces and tried to remember what it had been like for him at that age. He'd never worn jeans and T-shirts, that much he remembered vividly. And he certainly hadn't climbed on any of the furniture. He frowned. He did remember a pony on his sixth birthday. A clown on his seventh. He was too tired to remember the rest.

Dex eased his head back on the sofa. What difference did it make anyway? He couldn't change the past. Didn't even want to.

THE HOUSE was eerily quiet when Dex awoke. Quiet and dark, he noted as he rubbed his eyes. He sat up on the sofa, his arms and lap now empty. Where were the children? What time was it?

As if in answer to his unspoken question, the grandfather clock in the hall chimed the hour, falling silent after the eleventh resounding dong.

He switched on the table lamp at the end of the sofa and blinked to adjust to the light. How could he have slept through the children being taken from his arms? He obviously was more exhausted than he'd realized. He wondered, though, why no one had awakened him.

Dex stood and stretched. Since everyone else appeared to have gone to bed already, he might as well do the same. His stomach rumbled. He remembered then that he'd missed dinner. Surely he could find something in the kitchen. As he turned to leave the room something caught his eye. He turned back to the bookcases from which he'd rescued the twins and studied the fourth shelf of one in particular.

Photo albums.

A few steps later, he held two large albums in his hands. His heart started to pound again as he sat down and spread the albums on the coffee table before him. The first one held family photo after family photo. Pictures of the twins and the little princess. A smile stretched across his lips as he thought about their rapt attention as he'd read the story to them. He hadn't expected to feel that sense of protection, but he had. The idea that one of the boys could have been hurt climbing that bookcase had scared him witless. They weren't his children. He barely knew them. How could he feel that way?

Basic human compassion, he told himself, nothing more.

The next album he opened almost stopped his heart. Tara Cooper. Her Sweet Sixteen party. Dex swallowed tightly. She was beautiful. He touched the smiling face in the photograph. Blond hair fell around her shoulders. Bright hazel eyes flashed with happiness. The resemblance between her and his Grandmother Cooper was striking. And he'd been right about the smile. Their smiles were very similar, both wide, honest, heartfelt.

Dex turned the page and found a picture of Tara and a healthy-looking cow sporting a blue ribbon. He smiled. The next picture showed her winning yet another blue ribbon. This time from 4-H. He could barely make out the title of her poster: Better Nutrition, Eating Healthier and Leaner. He remembered then that Grandfather Cooper had said she'd wanted more, just like Ty.

He flipped another page. High-school graduation pictures. Visits home from college. Her twenty-first birthday. Her graduation from college. The elder Coopers looked so proud. He turned another page. A kind of shock rocked through him as his brain assimilated what his eyes saw next.

Tara Cooper and Charles Dexter Montgomery, Ju-

nior, together. So young…so happy. Dex was stunned
at the smiling face of his father. Every single photo
in the Montgomery house showed a solemn-looking
young man. The man in these pictures laughed,
hugged and played. Dex shook his head in bewilderment. Had his mother changed his father's life that
much? Had she been the one thing that made him
smile? Was that happiness what had distracted his father from the world the Montgomerys had so carefully
constructed in Atlanta?

Why had no one told him how happy his father
was during his brief marriage? Emotions twisting in
his chest, Dex turned to the next page. His hand shook
as he released it. His mother and father, tears of joy
glistening in their eyes, holding two tiny babies, captured forever in that one frozen frame in time. This
was his mother and father. He looked about the semi-
dark room. This had been their home. They'd been
happy here. And no one had ever told him that.

Unable to bear looking anymore, Dex closed the
albums. How could the Montgomerys have not known
how happy their son was here? Dex had always been
led to believe that even if the tragedy had not oc-
curred, his father would never have been happy with
his mother. Could they really have been that blind?

Dex pushed to his feet and carried the albums back
to the bookcase. Too many unanswered questions
whirled in his head. If he confronted the Coopers,
would they tell him the truth? Or would it merely be
their version of the truth? But then, they did have
photos to back them up. His father had been happy
here. There was no denying that fact. Could the Montgomerys say the same?

As Dex turned to go, he hesitated. As an after-thought, he flipped through one of the albums again until he came to the photo of his mother and father holding their newborn twins. Glancing around the room first, he slipped the photo from beneath its protective cover and tucked it into his pocket. He wanted this picture. He wanted to understand how fate could have torn such a lovely little family apart.

When he put the album back on the shelf something else captured his attention. Tucked way back in the corner behind a couple of fallen books he found a bundle of old letters. The once-white envelopes were yellowed and bound together by a pink ribbon. The return address was his own back in Atlanta. His heart started to pound all over again. His father had written these letters. He decided to take the letters as well. He swallowed and struggled for composure. He would read them, just not tonight. He wasn't sure he could take any more revelations tonight.

Dex climbed the stairs still reeling with the emotions of his discovery. He was too tired and too disturbed to care about eating or that hot bath he'd promised himself. He hid the letters in the top drawer of the bureau, peeled off his clothes and slid between the cool sheets of his bed. He wondered briefly how Ty was doing in Atlanta. Though he'd rather deny it, he missed his grandparents. Slowly, but surely, one smiling face after another belonging to the Cooper clan flashed through his mind. He felt the peaceful silence of the big old house as the family slept, the whole ambiance of the ranch and its inhabitants. They were two different worlds, this one and the one in which he'd grown up.

With no place to meet in the middle.

Dex didn't want to think about any of this any more. This wasn't home. These people were not his family.

There was nothing here he needed besides some answers.

The blue eyes and sweet smile of Leanne Watley protested his last thought. A warm, somehow softer feeling cloaked him. He told himself again that he didn't need her, either.

But she needed him.

Chapter Five

Leanne flipped through the rack of dresses once more. She didn't know why she tortured herself. She'd already selected the only one she even halfway liked that was in her price range. She might as well accept it as her dress for the dance. Mrs. Paula Beaumont, the owner and operator of Paula's Fashions, the only shop that sold anything besides denim and leather goods in Rolling Bend, had suggested it.

The pink color was pretty, though the design was a little plain. It fit a little too loosely, but Paula would make the necessary alterations. Leanne held the pink dress against herself once more and peered into the mirror. There had been a time when her mother could have made her a dress even prettier, but not now.

"That looks lovely, Leanne," Mrs. Paula said as she joined her near the mirror. "You can wear those white shoes you wore to church last Sunday with it."

Leanne frowned. She hadn't even thought about shoes. Her church shoes would have to do. She definitely couldn't buy new shoes, too. She wouldn't even be here looking at dresses if her mother hadn't insisted. She couldn't afford to buy a new dress. But her mother was right. She had nothing to wear.

"Don't you like it, dear?"

Leanne forced a smile. "Yes, ma'am," she said, dismissing her distracting thoughts. She hung the dress on the handy rack next to the mirror. "It's just that the blue one is so pretty." She glanced at the blue dress hanging alongside the pink one. A royal blue, the silky dress was beautiful.

Despite knowing she couldn't possibly afford a dress that cost more than a month's groceries, she'd tried it on anyway. The fabric had caressed her skin and hugged her figure in a most flattering way. The way the skirt swung about her legs when she moved made her giddy. Ty would like this dress. She was sure of it.

She sighed. Why on earth did it matter if he liked it or not? Why was she suddenly so concerned with looking good Friday night? Foolish, foolish, that's all.

"Oh, honey," Mrs. Paula offered with too much understanding in her eyes. "You're right, the blue dress is a pretty thing. But it's so expensive." She fingered the silken fabric. "And it really wouldn't be good for anything but the dance. It's a little too flamboyant for church, if you know what I mean."

It was true. The neckline of the blue dress was a little low, the shimmery material a little too flashy. Mrs. Paula was right. The dress was perfect for the dance. It would highlight Leanne's blue eyes. But it wasn't the sensible choice.

Mrs. Paula scooped up two handfuls of Leanne's hair and arranged it high on her head. "With that nice high collar on the pink dress it would look best to wear your hair up. And maybe a little flower right here.'' She gestured vaguely. ''You'd look really nice,'' she added as she released Leanne's hair and stepped back slightly. ''Pink is a good color on you, too.''

''You're right.'' Leanne nodded. ''I should stick with the pink one.'' Contrary to her words, she took the blue dress from the rack and held it against her one last time. It was so pretty. ''But I do love this one,'' she said softly, wistfully.

Mrs. Paula nodded, another understanding gesture. ''I'll ring the pink one up for you. I'm sure I can do the alterations this afternoon. I'll have Amos drop it by your house this evening. That okay?''

Leanne nodded without looking away from the mirror. When Mrs. Paula had left her alone, she turned side to side, swishing the material and taking in the look from every possible angle.

''I do love this dress,'' she murmured.

A long, low whistle sounded behind her, making Leanne jump. She whirled around to face the intrusion, the shimmering blue material swirling with her.

Ty.

Her breath caught. ''Ty,'' she choked out. ''What are you doing here? I thought your gran did all your Sunday-best shopping for you.''

He smiled, a gesture that made her heart thump wildly in her chest. ''I need a new shirt for Friday night.''

She nodded mutely.

His gaze swept her from head to toe and back. She saw the masculine approval there when those dark eyes focused on hers once more. Another breath trapped in her lungs.

"Wow," he said softly. "You look..." He seemed suddenly at a loss for words.

Leanne quickly hung the blue dress back on the rack. "I should be going. I have chores to do."

He looked from the blue dress to her. "You don't want it?"

He knew she did, she could see it in his eyes. How long had he been listening before he made his presence known?

She didn't need Ty feeling sorry for her. "No," she lied. "I've already made my selection."

She'd be willing to bet he'd already forgotten about his promise to help her with her plans for the ranch, too. It was so easy to be gallant with words. It was still difficult for her to believe that he'd meant what he said.

"Oh," he said almost contritely.

Since Ty'd come back from the city, he didn't act like himself at all. Where was the decisive man she'd known her entire life? Ty never waffled about his thoughts. His assessment that her dude ranch was a good idea had out and out shocked her. Ty believed ranches were for one thing and one thing only, raising cattle. What had motivated this sudden change of heart? Was he hoping that her dream would somehow help him convince his family that the two of them weren't right for each other?

Well, good. Because she didn't want to marry him anyway. Her temper flared. "Good day, Ty," she snapped as she started past him.

Strong fingers curled around one arm, effectively

halting her and at the same time drawing her nearer to him. "Did I say something wrong?" he asked softly. "I only meant that you would look stunning in the blue dress, that's all. It wasn't my intent to make you angry."

She looked up at him. Those dark, analyzing eyes made her shiver. He had never looked at her that way before, not that she could recall. She was certain she would remember that look.

"I didn't mean to be short with you," she said, sounding breathless. She prayed he wouldn't notice. He was still looking at her so very intently. "I...I have a lot of work to do."

His fingers tightened around her arm at the same instant something new flickered in that dark gaze. He released her but not before Leanne recognized what she saw—desire. Another shiver rushed over her. She hadn't imagined it. It was there. She'd seen it clearly.

"Stop by the hardware before you leave town," he instructed, easing back a step, putting some distance between them. "Leave a list of the things you need for painting and the other repairs."

Leanne almost smiled. He hadn't forgotten his promise. Deep down she'd known he wouldn't. Ty never made a promise he didn't intend to keep. But thinking negative thoughts helped her stay focused where he was concerned. It would be far too easy to fall head over heels in love with such a caring, honest man. But it wasn't what she wanted—not with Ty. They didn't see eye to eye on a wife's role in marriage. She knew what he wanted—a woman who would be happy at home raising his kids, and keeping house. She wanted more. Besides, she loved Ty like a brother.

Didn't she?

She suppressed the urge to shiver yet again. It was extremely difficult to think straight with him looking at her like that. She refused to call what she felt desire. It was probably just her subconscious reacting to the pressure of her mother's wish for her and Ty to marry. She'd spent a lifetime being an obedient daughter. Now she had no intention of doing anything except following her heart. As those dark eyes continued to peer deeply into hers, making her feel at once too warm and utterly restless, the only question that remained was, where was her heart taking her?

"All right," she finally said in response to his order to stop by the hardware. "I can't get it all at once, but I will give Mr. Dickson the list."

Ty nodded. "Good." He smiled again. Her pulse reacted. "How about helping me find something for the dance before you go? I wouldn't want to disappoint my date."

Date?

Leanne blinked. He considered Friday night's dance a date? "Well...ah...sure." She smoothed her suddenly damp palms over her denim-clad hips. "What did you have in mind?"

He shrugged. "I don't know. What would you suggest?"

"Well." Feeling suddenly bold, she took his hand in hers and dragged him toward the men's section. "Let's see what we can find."

When they reached a long rack of men's dress

shirts, Leanne shuffled through the offered selections. With his dark coloring she knew what she wanted.

"How about this one?" She held the long-sleeved white shirt against his broad chest.

Without even looking down, he said, "Perfect."

She blushed. "Don't you want to try it on? It might not fit."

He took the shirt from her and glanced around the store. "Sure, where's the dressing room?"

She angled her head toward the back of the store. "Back there, but there's someone using it right now. Mrs. Paula only has one dressing room, you know."

He thrust the shirt back at her. "No big deal. We'll just do as the Europeans do."

She frowned. "Europeans?" What in the world did that mean? Before Leanne could figure that one out, Ty had pulled his shirttail from his jeans and started unfastening the snaps. "What are you doing?"

He popped open the final snap of his shirt and dragged it off over impossibly wide shoulders. "I'm taking my shirt off," he said, nonchalantly.

Her eyes widened as all that sculpted terrain was bared before her. "I can see that." She glanced in Mrs. Paula's direction. The fiftyish, heavyset woman stood behind her counter, her mouth gaping. "Ty, you—"

He reached for the shirt she held, his fingers brushing hers as he took it from her. "You're sure this is the one you like best?"

She nodded, unable to speak or meet his eyes. She could only stare at that awesome chest. She'd seen him shirtless before. What made this time so different? He shouldered into the crisp white dress shirt and adjusted the collar. The stark contrast between his naturally tanned skin and the fresh white of the shirt took her breath away.

"It's...yes," she managed to say.

"What about a tie?" He reached behind her, making her heart stutter with his nearness. He dangled a black string tie near the hollow of his throat, drawing her rapt attention there. "What good's a white shirt without a black tie?"

She'd never known him to be so playful and talkative, not like this anyway. This was different. It was flirtatious. Sexy.

"You should definitely get the tie," she told him. His smile was contagious. She just couldn't help herself.

His expression grew serious. "You should do that more often. You have a beautiful smile."

She tried to think what to say, but no words would come. He felt closer suddenly, though she wasn't sure he'd moved.

"I have to go." The words had come from her, but she wasn't sure how she'd managed to say them.

He nodded. "Don't forget to stop by the hardware."

Before she could do something totally insane like kiss him again, Leanne rushed out of the shop. She didn't even stop at the counter to pay her bill.

Right now, she just had to get away from Ty. She told herself again that he was only a friend. One she'd known her whole life. He shouldn't be able to make her feel so flustered. So uncertain of what she really wanted.

Why would he? He'd never made her feel this attraction before. She'd always believed that he didn't want this arranged marriage any more than she did. So why was he suddenly behaving so strangely?

Leanne didn't understand it.

She wondered if Ty did.

Dex watched through the shop's plate-glass window as Leanne climbed into her old truck and drove away. A yearning so strong rose inside him that he couldn't take a breath for one long moment. He couldn't label it, didn't even understand it, but the feeling shook him as nothing else ever had. What was it about her that touched him so?

Deep in thought, he started to remove the shirt he'd tried on. A gasp startled him from his reverie. He stopped abruptly and turned to find the shop owner and another woman staring at him, wide-eyed, from their positions near the counter.

Knowing better, but suddenly not caring, Dex flagrantly, suggestively peeled off the white shirt, then took his time pulling on his own. One by one he fastened each snap, then tucked it into his waistband. When he'd finished, he winked at the ladies, earning himself another gasp from each.

He picked up the white shirt Leanne had selected and the black tie and headed for the cashier. One of the ladies grabbed her package and ran for the door. Dex grinned.

"Ty Cooper," Mrs. Paula scolded. "You did that on purpose. Your pa raised you better than that. Why, poor Mrs. Larkin will have to have one of her little nerve pills to calm down. I hope you think about that when you're sitting in church on Sunday and the reverend's talking about the evil sinners do."

Dex resisted the urge to tease her some more as he placed his selections on the counter. "I don't know what came over me," he offered contritely, with absolutely no sincerity. "I guess the devil made me do it."

The exasperation in the woman's voice when she spoke again was belied by the twinkle of mischief in her eyes. "I'm quite certain that you're right. It might promote business though. Perhaps you'd like to come by Saturday morning and model a few items." She cocked one eyebrow. "After all, if something good comes of the devil's work, the Lord might just overlook it."

"I'll check my calendar." Dex ran a hand through his hair, only then realizing he'd left his hat in his truck. He wondered if Ty would have been caught dead without it. Then again, he had a feeling Ty wouldn't have done a strip tease in the only fine clothing store in Rolling Bend.

Oh well. There was no telling what kind of fixes Ty was getting Dex into in Atlanta.

"Would you like me to put this on your account, Ty?" Mrs. Paula asked as she boxed his shirt and tie.

Dex considered that for a moment. He supposed that was the only way to go. He could reimburse Ty later. He definitely couldn't wear any of the shirts he'd found in Ty's closet to the dance. He'd found a pair of black jeans that would do.

As Dex signed Ty Cooper's name to the bill, he thought of the blue dress and the wistful sound of Leanne's voice when she'd said how much she loved it.

He hesitated only a split second. "What about that blue dress Leanne looked at?"

The lady shook her head. "Oh, it's far too expensive. Almost two hundred dollars. She's much better off with the pink one. What would Leanne do with a two-hundred-dollar dress?"

"But," Dex pressed, all business now, "it's the one she liked best, is it not?"

The shop owner looked taken aback. "Well, yes, but she has to be practical. The pink one will be good for church, too."

"The dress is for sale, isn't it?"

She nodded. "It's for sale, but…"

Dex looked her straight in the eye. "Put the blue one on my bill and deliver it to Leanne when you send her the pink one."

"Well…I…if you're sure that's what you want to do. It's an awful lot of money."

"I trust you'll take care of it?" he suggested.

"Of course." She passed him the package containing his purchases. "Anything else?"

"I think that takes care of everything." He winked at her. "Have a nice day."

She nodded uncertainly.

Dex pivoted and strode to the door. He suddenly wished he could be there to see the look on Leanne's face when the blue dress arrived. He smiled to himself. He could imagine just how pleased she would be. He frowned as he reached for the door handle. His actions this morning were so out of character. He couldn't say what had possessed him. If George were here perhaps he could explain what compelled Dex to make Leanne happy. He'd only known her for a few days, so why were her feelings so important to him?

Dex stepped back for two ladies to enter as he opened the door. They both stared at him, then giggled. He wondered what that was about. When the door closed behind him realization hit. The word of his little escapade was already spreading around town.

He slid into the seat behind the wheel of Ty's truck. His brother might not forgive him for tarnishing his stellar reputation. Dex grinned. Then again, the way he saw it, it would only add interest to a man who appeared to be far too reserved for his own good.

Dex considered that the same could be said about him. He was all business. Well, he amended, most of the time. He'd always been too busy for a real social life. Maybe he'd missed more than he realized. He'd certainly never dealt with everyday people as he had since his arrival here. He had a very efficient staff who took care of his needs. Maybe that was a mistake. Maybe he needed to be around people more.

Or maybe he just needed his head examined.

His Grandfather Montgomery would no doubt think so. Dex had been taught from a young age that appearances were everything. Power and respect could only be gained through the proper presentation.

It was about time he put that philosophy to the test.

Besides, it was all for naught. He was Ty Cooper right now.

Chapter Six

"All right, I'm giving you this one last chance." Dex looked the horse straight in the eye. "Don't push your luck. I'm out of patience."

Dex took the horse's silence as agreement. He walked around to the animal's left side as he had a half dozen times already, took a deep breath, placed his left foot in the stirrup and heaved himself upward the same way he'd watched Chad and Court do.

The horse sidestepped. Dex came down fast on his right foot, barely keeping his balance. He cursed loudly.

"Whatcha doing, Uncle Ty?"

He whipped around. Angelica stood near the barn door watching him. He'd have sworn the place was empty.

"I'm working with my horse."

Angelica studied him closely, as if trying to decide if he was telling the truth or not. "Why don't you call him Dodger no more? Did you decide to name him something else?"

Dodger. The horse's name was Dodger. That was

helpful. Maybe this kid could be useful for something other than throwing green beans at him.

"No, I like his name." Dex pushed his hat up and scratched his forehead. "Dodger seems to be mad at me right now. He doesn't want me to take him for a ride."

"You ain't doing it right." Angelica took a few steps in his direction. "You gotta grab the saddle horn when you go up. That's what my daddy does."

Dex frowned. How had he missed that? He lifted a skeptical eyebrow. "You're sure about that?"

"'Course." She adopted an impish grin. "You know that."

"Just checking to make sure you do."

"Ever'body knows that," she told him.

Dex assumed the position, grabbing the saddle horn this time. He went all the way up and into the saddle with little effort. He grinned. He'd done it.

"Toldcha."

Dex nodded. "So you did."

"Are you gonna go for a ride, Uncle Ty?"

He considered it. "Yes, I think I will."

"Can I go, too? My momma says I can ride as long as I'm with a grown-up."

He supposed it was the least he could do since she'd helped him out. But then, how was he supposed to get her into the saddle with him?

She climbed up onto a bale of hay. "Please?"

Dex guided the horse close to the hay bale, then reached for the child, lifting her into the saddle in front of him. "You're sure your mother won't mind?"

"'Course not. She knows you'll take good care of me."

Dex made the clicking sound he'd heard the other men make and Dodger started forward. "Where are we going, Princess?"

"How'd you know I was a princess?" she asked, giggling.

"Just a good guess."

Angelica waved to her mom who had stepped out onto the back porch to check on her child, Dex presumed. He waved, too. Grandmother Cooper peeked out next, waving and smiling. The gesture made him feel warm inside. It was foolish he knew, but he just couldn't help himself.

For the rest of afternoon, Dex and the princess rode around the ranch with her explaining everything they saw, just the way her father had explained it to her. Dex found all this very helpful. Now he wouldn't be so lost. It almost felt as if the child realized he needed a lesson about the ranch. But how could she?

By the time the dinner bell rang, Angelica had grown tired and all but fallen asleep in his arms. After taking care of the horse as he'd seen his brothers do, he carried the child to the house. When he climbed onto the porch, Lady wagged her tail. Dex paused, surprised.

"Good dog," he commented. He supposed that Lady considered him harmless enough if he'd made friends with one of the children—especially the princess.

Inside, Jenny, Angelica's mother, waited to take her daughter. "Let's get you washed up for supper, young lady."

As she ascended the stairs, the princess waved at Dex. He couldn't help a smile. He felt an unfamiliar shifting in his chest. He shook his head. A rugrat had stolen his heart. Unbelievable. Dex joined the men who were washing up in the kitchen. They'd been gone when he returned from town that morning. He wondered if they'd noticed he was missing.

"We missed you today, boy," his Grandfather Cooper said.

"I had some business in town," Dex offered, hoping that would be the end of it. Was he supposed to check in with his grandfather before leaving the ranch? Maybe there were certain tasks for which Ty was responsible.

"Mrs. Watley told your Gran that you'd offered to help Leanne get some work done over there." He clapped Dex on the back. "That's mighty good of you. We can handle things around here. You help Leanne out all you can. She's a good girl. The best."

Dex nodded, thankful for the reprieve. "I'll do that."

Court winked. "I think I hear wedding bells already," he teased.

"I know I do," Chad said as he dried his hands. "Guess Rolling Bend's about to lose its most eligible bachelor."

Dex felt heat rise up from his collar. "I just want to help her out," he assured Ty's brothers. "That's all."

"'Course you do," Court said with a laugh. "I saw the way you looked at her at dinner the other night. It was like you'd just laid eyes on her for the first time."

He had, but Dex didn't mention it.

"The next thing you know," Chad put in as they walked to the dining room, "you'll be hearing the pitter patter of little feet just like the rest of us."

The Coopers had him married and having children. Was this why Ty was all too willing to have some time away? The image of Leanne slipped into his head. The thought of her with Ty made his gut clench.

Dinner proved to be the usual Cooper clan experience. Lots of talk and laughter. Tonight's fare included fried pork chops, something the others called turnip greens, and baked beans. Like the green beans, the brown beans contained a large chunk of fatty meat. Seasoning, he'd determined.

"Did you have a nice ride with your Uncle Ty, Angel?" Chad asked his little girl.

Dex tensed. What if she told them about the episode in the barn or the fact that he'd gotten lost and she'd had to tell him the way back to the house?

She beamed a wide smile. "We had the bestest time. Uncle Ty promised to take me again real soon." She turned that mega-watt smile in his direction and gave him a little wink.

He'd promised her no such thing. The little black-mailer. "Anytime," he said, his smile matching her own.

The subject of the dance came up, then. The whole Cooper clan would be there. It was an annual tradition. Everyone sounded excited. The food was always great and the music loud, Dex learned.

He couldn't wait, he mused. It obviously took very little to excite these people.

"The dance is always a good time to make announcements,'' Grandfather Cooper commented aloud.

All eyes turned to Dex at the precise instant that a bean hit him in the chest.

Chad scolded his child while Dex grappled for something to say. ''I'm not sure I'll know anything from the investors by then,'' he said, pretending to believe that's what the older man was talking about.

''Well, maybe something *else* will come up.''

Dex smiled weakly at his grandfather. These people didn't give up. He wondered how Ty handled the situation.

''That was mighty generous of you to buy Leanne that nice dress,'' Grandmother Cooper said.

How did she know that? Dex swore silently. Small-town life. The whole place probably knew before sundown that he'd bought the dress. His mouth went dry at the thought that they might also know about his moment of temporary insanity.

''It was the one she wanted,'' he offered lamely.

Chad and Court hit a high five across the table. Dex felt like crawling under it.

''Agnes Washburn and Corine Miller said you put on quite a show in the shop,'' Brenda, Court's wife, suggested.

The brothers hee-hawed.

''Well, I...''

''You don't have to explain, son,'' Grandfather Cooper hastened to put in. ''It's spring, you're in love.''

''In heat,'' one of the brothers muttered.

Dex glared at both of them.

''That's enough of that,'' Grandmother Cooper

chided. She smiled at Dex. Her smile played havoc with his equilibrium.

Another bean flew in his direction, drawing Dex's attention back to the little princess.

He was in real trouble here, he admitted.

Ty would kill him when he came back. The whole family now believed him in love with Leanne. Angelica clearly suspected something. And the whole town was talking about his lack of modesty at the clothing store.

"I'm sorry just to barge in."

Dex looked up in time to see Leanne burst into the room. She looked angry—and beautiful.

"Join us," Grandmother Cooper offered. "You know you're always welcome here, dear."

Leanne shook her head. "I can't stay long. I just need to talk to Ty a moment." She glared at him. "Alone."

Bewildered and suddenly wary, Dex rose from the table. "Excuse me," he murmured out of habit.

He followed Leanne from the dining room, the sound of muffled laughter and throats clearing echoing behind him.

Outside on the porch she rounded on him. "How dare you," she demanded.

How dare he what? "Pardon me?"

She narrowed her gaze at him. "Don't play dumb with me, Ty Cooper. You know what you did."

He frowned, trying to figure out what she could possibly mean. "Would you like to let me in on exactly what you're accusing me of?"

She set her hands on her hips and glared up at him, fury snapping in those pretty blue eyes. "I bought the dress I wanted to wear to the dance. How dare you buy the blue one and send it to me!''

His confusion deepened. "I thought you liked the blue one.''

She tossed her head, sending long blond tresses over her shoulder. "Of course I like it, but that's not the point. I bought the pink one. If I'd wanted the blue one I would have bought it. I don't need your charity.''

Oh, so that's what this was about. "It wasn't charity," he said evenly.

"Then what was it?''

"It was a gift.''

She huffed out a breath, but some of her fury had dissipated. "A gift? What for? It's not my birthday.''

He crossed his arms over his chest. "For no special reason. I wanted you to have it.''

Her temper flared again. "I don't need your sympathy, either.''

He smiled. He couldn't help himself. She was truly gorgeous when her temper flared. "Do you know how beautiful you are when you're angry?" He shook his head, scarcely believing his own words. But they were true. He'd gone this far, he might as well finish what he'd started. "Your eyes light up and your cheeks flush." His gaze settled on that lush mouth. "It's amazing," he murmured.

She took a step closer to him and shook her finger in his face. "Are you trying to seduce me?''

That question sent a jolt of shock through him. "What? Seduce you? No. I...''

"Then what was all that about this morning, undressing in front of me?''

Was that going to haunt him forever? "I wasn't trying to seduce you," he protested. "I just didn't think. I—" He shrugged. "I don't know why I did it." Had he been trying to seduce her? He resisted the urge to shake his head again. That didn't make sense. Why would he—?

"Well, you shouldn't have behaved so...so forward," she said and sniffed as if incensed.

A theory nagged at Dex. "Methinks the lady doth protest too much," he said, the concept gaining momentum.

She shot him a seething gaze. "What does that mean?"

"It's simple," he said, leaning forward, going nose to nose with her. "I tried the shirt on because it was necessary. If the act turned you on," he shrugged again. "Well, there's nothing I can do about that."

Fury blazed in those baby blues. "Don't flatter yourself. There's absolutely nothing about you that would turn me on."

His competitive nature stirred instantly. "Oh yeah?"

"Yeah."

"Then why is your heart beating so fast?" He had her there. He could see the pulse fluttering wildly at the base of her throat.

She didn't miss a beat. "Because I'm madder than hell, that's why, you...you jerk."

"And just a little turned on?" he insisted. *He* sure as hell was. His radar couldn't be that far off.

She surprised him. "So what if I am a little turned on? Big deal. It doesn't mean **anything**." She lifted her chin defiantly. She thought she had him there.

"Really?"

"That's right." She looked him up and down. "You're not exactly unaffected yourself."

She did have him there. It wasn't like he could hide it. "Prove it," he challenged.

Her gaze shot to his. "Prove what?" A good deal of her bravado dissolved right before his eyes.

"That it's nothing…that I only turn you on just a little." Oh, he was feeling really wicked now. Wicked and far too excited to think rationally.

She looked uncertain, but not quite ready to back down. "And just how am I supposed to do that?"

"Kiss me."

Her eyes widened. "What?"

"Kiss me. If it doesn't do anything for you, then you've proven your point."

"Good night," she said, her voice clipped as she brushed past him.

"Guess I was right, then," he said, smiling in triumph.

She whirled around, shooting him a drop-dead stare. "You are not right."

"Yes, I am."

Fury glittering in her eyes, she marched straight up to him, grabbed him by the shirt, jerked him down to her and kissed him hard on the mouth.

His mouth claimed hers. Her palms flattened against his chest. When she would have pushed him away, he drew her closer. His arms tightened around her tiny waist, aligning her body with his. She felt soft against him, and so very fragile. But her kiss was like fire. Her mouth full, soft, hungry. Her hands moved up and over his chest until her arms wrapped around his neck. She tiptoed then, pressing her hips more fully into his and creating a whirlwind of sensation inside him. He groaned.

The kiss went on forever. If he'd ever kissed a woman this innocent yet this eager, he had no recall of it. His body hardened to the point of pain. He wanted more than she would be willing to give, he was certain of that. But he would take this one moment.

She drew back, her face flushed, her eyes glazed with lust. "Stop," she whispered, breathless.

He couldn't help himself, and he kissed those full, wet lips once more. "Admit it," he murmured against her lips, "and I'll stop."

"You win." She stepped away from him, then swayed. He steadied her. "Satisfied?" Anger burned away the lust in her eyes.

"Not by a long shot." He cupped her face in his hands and kissed her once more before she could stop him. This time, he thrust his tongue inside that luscious mouth. She whimpered at the feel of him inside her. When he'd had his fill of exploring that hot little mouth, he drew back. "Now I'm satisfied."

She jerked from his grasp and rushed away before he could say good-night. The truck's engine roared to life and she spun away in a spray of dust and gravel.

Dex watched her go, his body still humming with desire. He'd made a mistake. He closed his eyes and shook his head. A huge mistake.

He'd tasted heaven and now he wanted it.

But he wasn't Ty Cooper.

He couldn't let lust sweep them away when she had no idea who he really was.

It wouldn't be right.

And no matter how many one-night stands he'd had in the past without looking back, he had a feeling she wasn't the kind of woman a man walked away from so easily.

EVEN AFTER a long hot bath Leanne couldn't relax enough to go to sleep. Instead she paced her room like a caged animal. She should never have allowed Ty to goad her into that first kiss. She closed her eyes and steadied herself when the flood of sensations that accompanied the memory overwhelmed her. The feel of his firm mouth on hers. The feel of his strong, lean body, hard with need for her, pressed against hers made her weak with want.

Leanne forced her eyes open, and thoughts of Ty away. She couldn't feel this way. She didn't want to marry him and be the kind of rancher's wife he wanted…needed. But she couldn't imagine why she suddenly had all these crazy mixed-up feelings for him. It didn't make sense. A week ago she'd felt nothing more than sisterly feelings for him. Now, suddenly, she couldn't sleep for thinking of him. Whenever he was near her heart raced, her pulse leapt. And after those kisses, she wasn't sure of anything anymore. She crossed her arms over her chest.

What had happened to her?

She stared at the shimmering blue dress hanging on her closet door. What had possessed him to buy it for her? Ty had never shown any interest like that for her in the past. They'd been friends, practically family. Now he was buying her fancy dresses and trying to seduce her. It just didn't make sense.

Leanne plopped down onto the bed. He had promised to help her with the guest cabins. Another unexpected gesture. Not that he wouldn't have helped in the past if she'd asked, but this was different. Somehow. God, it was just too confusing. She couldn't think straight.

What if he decided not to help her?

She chewed her lip. No, that couldn't be. Ty never went back on his word. But then, Ty never did any of these other things, either. Maybe he was going through some sort of change here. Maybe...

She'd just have to wait and see if he showed up tomorrow morning. If he did, she'd have to be careful to keep things platonic. No more hot kisses. No more touching.

She flopped over onto her side and pulled her knees to her chest. Getting the guest cabins and the pool ready to use were the most important things right now. She couldn't get caught up in anything else.

The dance.

How would she get through a whole night with him at the dance? Working together was one thing, but a date—and he'd called it a date—was entirely different.

The telephone rang. Leanne shot to her feet. She had to get to it before it woke her mother. She ran downstairs, two stairs at a time, not slowing to consider who would be calling her at this time of night. It was almost midnight.

She grabbed the receiver on the fourth ring. ''Hello.''

''Leanne?''

Ty.

She pressed her hand to her chest and tried to catch her breath despite the racing of her heart. "Yes."

"I know it's late but I felt compelled to call." Silence stretched for several seconds. "I wanted to apologize for antagonizing you tonight. I behaved despicably. I hope you'll forgive me."

She frowned. The voice was his, but the words were all wrong. "Ty?"

"Y-yes," he said hesitantly. "I didn't want you to be angry with me."

She shook her head. "I'm not angry with you." She hesitated. "Not really. I just don't understand what's happening," she said in all honesty.

"I'm sure it's nothing," he said, his words wielding a hurt she hadn't expected. "Why don't we forget the whole incident?"

She blinked furiously, surprised to find moisture gathering in her eyes. "It's forgotten already," she said hollowly.

"Good." He hesitated again. "I'll see you tomorrow, then."

"Tomorrow," she echoed, barely retraining the tears. This was crazy. She blinked some more.

"Good night, Leanne."

"Good night, Ty."

She hung up.

It was nothing.

Then why did it suddenly feel like everything?

Chapter Seven

Dex parked in front of the Watley house the next morning at 8:00 a.m. Another sleepless night had left him with a less-than-amiable disposition. The kisses he'd stolen from Leanne had played havoc with his ability to relax. But with the phone call he'd made sure there was no misunderstanding. That was the last thing either of them needed. They could just start fresh today. He was here to help her, not seduce her. It had just happened. He was certain of it.

Today, like the days to follow, would be about work, about making her dream come true. Nothing else. Well, nothing else but keeping him off the Circle C.

At least here he was on steadier ground. He didn't know any more about painting than he did about running a ranch, but maybe he could do a better job of faking the former. Fighting his attraction to Leanne would certainly be simpler than enduring the Coopers' matchmaking schemes.

He remembered to retrieve his Stetson from the seat as he climbed out of the truck. Maybe painting would be a good excuse not to wear it. He could hope.

As he was about to climb the steps to the porch, Leanne came around the corner of the house. "Morning."

He nodded, instantly taking in the fit of her pink blouse and figure-forming jeans. "Good morning."

"My mother's resting. I don't want to disturb her, so if you don't mind I've already started around back."

"All right."

He settled the frustrating hat atop his head and followed her. Maybe he should be leading the way, he mused, since he couldn't keep his gaze off her swaying hips. Her long blond ponytail kept time with the rhythmic movement. He sighed, more loudly than he'd intended. She glanced over her shoulder, but didn't smile. He wondered if she could possibly know what he'd been thinking.

"I started on this one." She motioned to the cabin closest to the house.

When they entered the small cabin Dex was surprised that it was a good deal roomier inside than it looked. The one empty room was large enough to accommodate the appropriate living-room and bedroom furnishings. On the far wall was a small efficiency kitchen. On another wall there were two doors, one to a closet, one to a bathroom.

Dex's gaze settled on the two buckets of paint and the paint-filled pan sitting on the floor next to them. He frowned. "Did you pick up all the supplies we would need?"

"Two gallons of paint, one pan, a roller and handle and two paint brushes," she said triumphantly.

"What about the rest?" She would need a great

deal more than that to complete all the work. He might not be a painter by trade, but even he recognized that much.

"I told you I couldn't get it all at once," she countered, an edge in her voice. "This should keep us plenty busy today."

The money thing again, he realized, annoyed. "Come with me." He walked outside, then retraced the path they'd taken around the house. Dex tried to tamp down his impatience, but the effort proved futile. He preferred that his orders were followed without question, but she couldn't know that. She thought he was Ty. Somehow that disturbed him even more, but he pushed the sensation away. He was here to help and to avoid making obvious mistakes on the Circle C, not to become infatuated with a woman who didn't even know him.

"Where are you going?" she asked, walking fast to match his stride.

"*We* are going into town to pick up the necessary materials to do the job properly."

"Wait."

He ignored her as his impatience quickly turned to irritation. He liked things done in an efficient manner. He hated wasting his time. He suppressed the urge to wonder what Ty was doing in *his* office. Grandfather Montgomery would never allow him to make a bad business maneuver. Dex could count on that. But he wasn't supposed to be thinking about any of that right now. He was supposed—

Leanne grabbed him by the arm and turned him around, effectively halting him and his thoughts. He wanted to be angry, but the electricity her touch generated startled him, reminding him of last night's kiss. Fortunately, he recovered swiftly enough. "What is it now?" he demanded.

"I told you I can't buy everything at once."

"I didn't ask you to," he said just as pointedly.

"Ty," she countered.

For the first time since his arrival, the urge to correct her was nearly overwhelming. Whenever a Montgomery made up his mind, he didn't like being detained.

"Get into the truck, Leanne. Don't argue. Just do it." When she hesitated, he added, "When you told me what you wanted to do, I got the impression this was really important to you. Was I wrong?"

The stand-off lasted about three seconds. "You weren't wrong."

"Then get in."

She rounded the hood and climbed into the truck. Dex breathed a sigh of relief. One hurdle down. He didn't want to consider how many more to go.

MR. DICKSON at the Rolling Bend hardware store was more than happy to help. The first order of business was getting Leanne out of the store. Dex needed to speak privately with Mr. Dickson as soon as he determined it was safe to do so.

"Haven't done much painting, have you, Ty?" Mr. Dickson commented, amusement twinkling in his eyes.

Dex shook his head. "Someone else usually takes care of that task."

Mr. Dickson nodded. "Yeah, I was thinking Court was the painter in the Cooper family. Could make a living at it if he had the time and the inclination to leave the cattle business.''

Dex tried not to look too relieved that he wasn't expected to know more about this than he did. ''This is everything we'll need?'' he asked, determined to get on with it.

''That's it.'' Mr. Dickson crossed his arms and looked pleased with his large sale.

Dex glanced at the door to make sure Leanne wasn't back yet. ''Can you give me a quick block of instruction?'' He looked covertly from side to side. ''I'd prefer not to look completely inept. Do you know what I mean?''

Mr. Dickson winked at him. ''I understand completely. You don't want to look dumb in front of the little lady. I've impressed a few in my time.''

Dex nodded slowly. ''Right.''

During the fifteen minutes that followed, Dex received a quick lesson in ''do-it-yourself'' painting. It sounded easy enough. Especially the rolling part. The edging part that needed to be done with a brush sounded a bit more complicated. He'd leave that to Leanne. She had surely done some sort of painting in the past. If she'd painted her nails, she had more experience with a brush than Dex.

Before Leanne returned from the bakery and the other errands Dex had sent her on, he'd loaded the truck with the supplies they needed to get the job done.

She stared, aghast, at his purchases stacked in the bed of the truck. She waved the white bag from the bakery, being careful not to tip the tray containing two cups of coffee in the other hand. "What is all this?"

Dex pushed up his hat and swiped his damp brow. He couldn't recall ever having perspired quite like this unless he was on a racquetball court. "What we'll need to complete the job," he told her bluntly.

She shook her head. "I can't afford all this."

He took the tray. "We'll work that out later. Right now we have to get down to business." Why did she always question his instructions? He was doing this to help her.

When he got into the truck she followed suit, still looking a bit dazed. He already knew from experience how she felt about charity. He wasn't about to tell her that he had no intention of accepting repayment. To his way of thinking, she was doing him a favor getting him away from the ranch, even if it did give the wrong impression to the Coopers. At least they weren't suspicious about his reasons for staying away.

"Ty, I can't do this," Leanne announced after a few minutes of riding in silence. "I don't know when I'll be able to repay you. It wouldn't be right not to tell you that up front."

He thought about that for a minute, then decided upon an idea he hoped would satisfy her. "I have a couple of friends who could use a few days away from the city. Maybe you'd let them be your first guests."

"As repayment for all this?" She held his gaze when he glanced in her direction, uncertainty in her own.

"If you feel that's right."

She considered his suggestion for a few moments.

"Sounds fair." She stared straight ahead for a time, then asked the question he hadn't considered. "What friends? You've never mentioned any friends in the city before."

Dammit. He hadn't thought of that. "Just a couple of people I met when I went to Chicago," he said quickly. "No one I would have mentioned before."

"Oh."

Good save, he thought, relieved. Pretending to be someone else was a less than pleasant business.

"When would they want to come?" she continued, determined to nail him down on the details.

"Whenever you're ready to open for business."

"They could come, just like that?" She snapped her fingers. "Without notice?"

Dex couldn't tell her that it was two of his hospital administrators he had in mind, people who could adjust their schedules whenever he told them to.

"Sure." He left it at that in hopes she would leave it alone.

When he turned down the long drive that led to the Watley ranch and she hadn't asked any more questions, he decided she was satisfied.

Another hurdle behind him.

Who would have thought this Good Samaritan stuff was so complicated? Most women liked having money spent on them. The dress he'd bought Leanne, for example. He'd spent more than that on dinner and champagne for a date and never once had a complaint. He braked to a stop in front of her house and shoved the gear shift into Park. He just didn't get Leanne Watley. She wasn't like any woman he'd ever known. The memory of her taste broadsided him. His fingers tightened on the steering wheel. He had to stop allowing that to happen.

"Your *decaffeinated* coffee." She offered him a cup and smiled as he dragged his gaze in her direction.

His heart foolishly skipped a beat. "Thanks," he said, shaken.

"I didn't know you preferred decaf," she said, looking away.

Another misstep. "I guess I didn't know it either until I tried it while I was in Chicago."

"Seems like a lot of things changed while you were in Chicago," she said, the words almost too softly spoken to hear.

Dex tensed. Was she suspicious or simply surprised? He opened his mouth to offer an explanation but she spoke again before he could.

"I hope you know how much this means to me, Ty."

It was his turn to smile then, brittle though it might be. "I think I do. I have dreams, too."

"Like finding a larger market for selling your cattle?"

"That's one." He sipped the decaffeinated brew.

The bag rustled as she opened it and then offered him one of the pastries he'd asked her to pick up.

"Maybe later." He really wasn't hungry. Not for pastries, anyway. He forced his gaze straight ahead. No lustful thoughts, Montgomery, he reminded himself.

Looking thoughtful, she refolded the bag. "What's another one?"

He studied her for a moment, knowing full well it

was a mistake. "Another what?" The thread of conversation had vacated his brain.

"Dream," she prodded.

Oh, yes. He'd stepped right into that one. But what could it hurt to tell her the truth? He exhaled a heavy breath and stared out at the wide-open Montana sky. He wondered how any sky could be that blue. Like her eyes, he thought, turning back to her. Like nothing else he'd ever seen. "Making my grandfather proud is one of my goals." He sipped his coffee. "Dream, if you'd prefer the term."

Her forehead lined with confusion. "But he is proud. He's about the proudest grandpa I know."

Well, that hadn't worked out as he'd thought it would. He scowled. How to get out of this one? He shrugged. "I guess I'm not as sure of that as you are."

"Ty, that's ridiculous." She opened the passenger-side door and scooted out. "You're being too hard on yourself."

He got out as well. That wasn't the first time he'd been accused of being too hard on himself. His valet, George told him that all the time. "Maybe so," he offered in hopes of ending the discussion.

"Do you ever wonder what life would be like if your mother and father were still alive?"

That question stopped him cold. He wasn't sure how to answer. He thought about the letters he'd found and the picture in his wallet. The one he looked at every chance he got when he was sure no one was watching. What if they had lived?

"I'm sorry." She placed a hand on his arm, sending another little zing of electricity through him. "I shouldn't have asked that. It was thoughtless."

"No, it wasn't thoughtless. I do wonder about that sometimes." He leaned against the front of the truck and stared at the cup in his hand as if it held all the answers. "I wonder how my life would have been different. Where I might be right now. If I'd have any brothers and sisters."

She nodded, those pretty blue eyes solemn. "It's so sad. They were such a beautiful couple. I've looked at their pictures a hundred times. But your grandparents have loved you as if you were their own," she offered. "Chad and Court have been like brothers to you."

He looked away. If only that were true. "Yeah, I know you're right. I should just be glad for what I have." Regret trickled through him. Maybe he was being too hard on his Grandfather Montgomery. Dex had no way of knowing how the decision had been made thirty-two years ago. This whole charade could be a huge mistake.

"I know you miss your twin brother," she said softly.

He frowned, uncertain of that ground. How was it that everyone else had known that there were two and he hadn't? Even Ty had known that part, even if he didn't know Dex was alive. Dex had been completely isolated from all this. The twinge of regret he'd felt faded instantly.

"I hadn't missed him until recently," he said in all honesty.

"It's a shame he was lost, too." She shook her head. "Mom said that when your folks came back from their visit down south they grieved for months over having lost your brother while they were away." Her brow lined thoughtfully. "I always wondered but didn't want to ask why they didn't bring him back here to be buried." She shrugged. "I guess the loss was too devastating."

Lost? He'd been lost all right. Ire rushed through him, scorching away all other emotion. And he had every intention of seeing that the people responsible for this ridiculous scheme answered for their manipulation.

"A real shame," he agreed. It seemed like a safe enough response and gave no hint of the emotions roiling inside him. He had somehow to sort them out. He didn't like how they made him feel.

"So," she said cheerily, "where do we start, boss?"

Now *there* was something he could do, give instructions. He'd always been good at that.

"Cabin One," he suggested, seeing that the cabins weren't numbered yet. "Or are you going to call them by names?"

"I haven't decided. But we'll go with numbers for the time being. This way," she said with a dramatic sweep of her arms. Another of those pulse-tripping smiles spread across her pretty face.

Dex had hoped she would lead the way again. He liked nothing better than watching that heart-shaped derriere sway from side to side. He'd never known a woman who walked quite like that. He was learning all kinds of new things from this sweet country girl.

He just had to remember one important point, the

last thing she needed was a big, bad wolf like him. And right now he was definitely feeling wolfish.

Like a wolf who'd lied to her from the moment he'd laid eyes on her.

LEANNE TRIED her best to stay focused on the painting, but she couldn't help stealing glances at Ty. She closed her eyes and shook her head. What was it that suddenly drew her so to him? Had the years of prodding from her mother and the Coopers finally kicked in?

Whatever the case, she was too close to seeing her dream come true to throw it away now. No matter how nice Ty was to help her, he would not want his wife running a dude ranch. He would want her at home having babies like Court's and Chad's wives. Not that Leanne didn't want her share of babies. She did. Just not right now. She had plenty of time to think about marriage and children. Plenty.

Her gaze stole over to Ty once more. He'd rolled up his shirtsleeves and was working diligently on his second wall. The first had been a little tough going. Leanne had kept her mouth shut, but she hadn't missed his irritation until he got the hang of things. The task appeared to be moving smoothly now. She smiled as she considered that he literally had paint all over him. He even had it in his hair.

But it in no way detracted from his good looks. The man was definitely fine. She sighed softly. Broad, broad shoulders. Those muscled arms. Oh, and gosh, that awesome chest. The ladies around town were probably still talking about how he had bared that spectacular chest in Mrs. Paula's shop.

She would never forget that little show, Leanne mused dreamily. She couldn't help but wonder if the rest of him looked that magnificent. She frowned, trying to remember the last time she'd seen him in swimming trunks or cutoffs. Oh, and the man could kiss as well. Despite being twenty-three, she'd only been kissed a couple of times, and chastely at that. No one, *no one* had ever kissed her the way Ty had last night.

Another less pleasant memory, followed by an instant flash of fury chased away the tingling sensation the recall of his kisses evoked. He'd said it was nothing. So why should she tingle when she remembered it? She shouldn't. It was nothing.

She thunked her brush down onto the top of the paint can. It was almost noon. The least she could do was feed him. Of course, at the moment, she couldn't say if she cared whether he was hungry or not. ''I'll get lunch,'' she announced without preamble or manners and started out of the room.

He placed his paint roller in its tray and turned to her before she could get away. ''I should wash up.''

There was no denying that. Despite her irritation, Leanne couldn't stop the grin that tickled her lips when she looked at him. His arms were sprinkled with white splotches. He'd smeared paint on his left cheek and there was at least two spots in his hair. His clothes would never be the same.

''You find this amusing?'' He wasn't smiling, though she could see the amusement in his eyes.

Laughter bubbled into her throat. ''I'm sorry. It's just that you look so funny.''

One dark eyebrow arched, lending a devilish look

to his handsome face. "Just point me in the direction of soap and water."

Ty followed her into the house. Leanne fully expected to find her mother waiting at the kitchen table. Instead she found lunch already prepared. Sandwiches and chips, even freshly made lemonade.

"Make yourself at home," she said to Ty. "I need to check on Mom."

He mumbled something but the spray of water from the faucet muffled his words. As she headed into the hall, Leanne resisted the impulse to look back and see if he would take off his shirt again.

Her mother watched television from a comfortable mound of pillows propped up on the couch. Her hands were busy with knitting needles. It was the first time her mother had bothered with her knitting in months.

"Thanks for making lunch, but you didn't have to do that." Leanne sat in the chair next to her.

"I feel pretty good today." Joanna smiled, another very rare thing these days.

Seeing that smile on her mother's face made Leanne feel lightheaded. "That's wonderful. Would you like to join us for lunch?"

"Oh, no. I've already eaten." She waggled her eyebrows. "Besides, the two of you don't need an old stick-in-the-mud like me intruding on your time together."

Leanne didn't bother telling her mother that it wasn't what she thought. She didn't dare do anything to bring those high spirits down.

"All right, then. If you need anything we'll be working in the cabin closest to the house today."

She nodded. "I know. I saw you through the

kitchen window when you were unloading your supplies.'' She sighed. ''I swear, that Ty gets more handsome every day.''

Leanne kissed her mother on the cheek and took her time getting back to the kitchen. Why didn't she just go ahead and marry him? Being Ty's wife certainly wouldn't be a hardship. He might let her run the dude ranch. He certainly hadn't spoken against it when she'd told him about it.

She sighed. No, she wasn't in love with Ty. She wanted to be madly, truly, deeply in love with the man she spent the rest of her life with. Though she cared deeply for Ty, and even felt attracted to him lately, he just didn't make her heart flip-flop the way she'd dreamed her Prince Charming would.

Oh, he'd made it beat a little faster, that was true enough. But it just wasn't the way she knew it could be with the one man who was meant for her—with the man of her dreams, the one who had the power to make her forget all else.

Pushing the foolish thoughts away, she reentered the kitchen, producing a smile for her guest.

Ty stood before the sink, his back to her. Leanne stalled just inside the door.

He was naked from the waist up again. Shirtless and with his jeans riding low on his hips, his smooth skin glistened with water droplets. While she watched, he bent forward and splashed water on his face, then pushed his damp hands through his thick, dark hair. He straightened and turned away from the sink. Rivulets of water raced down his sculpted chest to soak into the waistband of his low-slung jeans.

Mesmerized, she watched as he dried his face and

upper body. Her mouth went dry and her breath left her lungs with each stroke of the terry cloth. But it was her heart that reacted the strongest. It flip-flopped, hard, in her chest.

Just then Ty opened his eyes. He smiled at her. Not just any old kind of smile. But one that said, *I know your heart just did a double somersault, and I'm about to make it do the same thing all over again. And again after that.*

Her heart did just that.

Just the way she'd dreamed it would.

Chapter Eight

Dex jerked the tie loose and retied it. His fingers just didn't seem to want to do what he wanted them to. He stared at his seemingly useless hands and frowned. His skin was dry, callused almost. He'd had to scrub like hell to get all the paint off. His left arm ached from overuse. It just wasn't natural to him, but he'd had to keep up the act down to the last detail, just in case. He blew out a frustrated breath and dropped his hands to his sides. The whole week had been like this. Everything he did, everything he said, came out wrong. He'd never felt so clumsy in his whole life. It just didn't make sense.

Sure it did, a little voice told him. It made perfect sense. He was in lust with Leanne Watley.

"Dammit."

"I'm gonna tell," a little voice singsonged from the open bedroom doorway. "Uncle Ty said a bad word."

Dex glared down at Angelica. "Go away."

She hugged her doll and swished back and forth, apparently enjoying the sound of lace against the stiff fabric of her dress. "If you don't take me for 'nother ride on your horse, I'll tell," she warned, making a little song out of the threat.

The child had been blackmailing him all week. He'd been forced to submit to her every whim. But he'd had enough. He leaned down nose-to-nose with her. "So tell," he challenged. "See if I care."

Angelica harrumphed, then whirled in a flurry of white lace and taffeta. "Mommy!" she shouted as she ran down the hall. "Uncle Ty's been gotted by aliens!"

Dex heaved a disgusted sigh. "Great," he muttered. He and Angelica needed to have a talk.

The kid was entirely too much like him. She didn't quit until she got what she wanted.

A scream rent the air. Dex bolted in the direction of the sound. Surely a simple swear word didn't warrant that kind of reaction. He skidded to a halt outside the open bathroom door. Jenny, Chad's wife and Angelica's mother, stood in the middle of the room, something he couldn't identify in her hand, Angelica standing next to her, staring upward in confusion.

"Oh, God, Ty," Jenny cried, her eyes bright. "It turned blue!"

· Dex frowned. "What turned blue?" he asked cautiously.

She waved the thing in her hand. "The stick!" She waved it again. "This! I'm pregnant!" She stared down at her little girl then. "We're going to have a baby!" She tossed the stick into the sink and grabbed Angelica in a big hug. "You'll have a little brother or sister."

Dex's frown slowly slipped upright into a smile.

She was going to have a baby. "You're pregnant!" he said lamely.

Jenny nodded, tears rolling down her cheeks. "We've tried for so long." She let go of her daughter and rushed to hug him. "I'm so happy."

He hugged her back. "That's great." Something like pride or maybe happiness bloomed in his chest. "That's so great." He patted her awkwardly.

She drew back. "I have to find Chad!"

She rushed down the hall, leaving a stunned Dex and an equally stunned Angelica. When Jenny had disappeared down the staircase, he glanced down at the princess.

Her doll forgotten on the bathroom floor, she planted her little fists on her hips. "Well, what if I don't wanna baby brother or sister?" She made a face. "Got too many babies around here now."

Oh, this was good. The little princess was jealous. "Get used to it, kid. Once the stick turns blue there's no stopping it."

Dex pivoted and strode back to his room. He'd loved to hang around and see how the princess handled her dilemma, but he had other things to do.

Like picking up the prettiest girl in the whole state of Montana. He fiddled with his tie, finally accomplishing his goal of tying it this time. Working with Leanne for the last three days had done nothing to lessen his hunger for another taste of her. But she'd kept her distance. He hadn't missed the flicker of desire in her eyes once or twice, but she didn't get too close. That was a good thing, he decided.

He couldn't understand what precisely it was about

that sweet little country girl that drove him to distraction, but whatever it was, he couldn't get enough.

Dex stared at his reflection. The image of Ty Cooper stared back. The bottom dropped out of his stomach. No matter how much he wanted Leanne he couldn't allow their relationship to go beyond the kissing stage. Her desire was for Ty, not him. He had to remember that. The truth would soon come out. He didn't want to hurt Leanne.

He didn't want to hurt any of them.

He pulled his wallet from his jeans and slipped the photograph of his mother and father out of it. This family had opened their arms to his father, had loved his mother desperately. Whatever their reasons for allowing him and Ty to be separated, he couldn't permit his own actions to hurt them in any way. Make them regret, maybe, but that was the extent of the retribution he required from the Coopers. He still didn't know how he felt about his Grandfather Montgomery's deception. He would deal with that soon enough. But not tonight. Tonight he was going to relax and enjoy being a Cooper.

Who knew? His stay here could end at any time. If Ty was discovered or if *he* was, the gig would be up.

He glanced at the bureau drawer where he'd hidden the letters. A yearning welled inside him. Maybe they held the answers he sought. Soon. Very soon, he promised himself. He intended to open them and see. He'd struggled with the idea of breaching his father's privacy, but he had to know the truth.

A few minutes later Dex shook his Grandfather Cooper's hand and kissed his grandmother's cheek before leaving to pick up Leanne. The whole family would be at the dance, but he felt like showing them some affection. He almost laughed at the idea that maybe the Cooper way was rubbing off on him already.

But, he considered as he drove toward Leanne's, he couldn't quite dispel the hint of bitterness he felt over the choices they had made. He would clear the air on that score soon enough. Dex parked near the Watley house and dismissed that line of thinking. Tonight he was going to have some fun, Montana style. He forced away thoughts of his Grandfather Montgomery's constant warnings about money-hungry women. Leanne was about as far from that as a woman could get.

Leanne was out the door by the time he reached the top step. He'd known the blue dress would complement her angelic features and those big blue eyes, but he hadn't expected this. She was beautiful. Truly, extraordinarily beautiful.

Her thick blond tresses fell around her shoulders like shining silk. The dress clung to her womanly figure in all the right places. His entire body tensed as his gaze lingered on her full breasts. She was perfect.

"Stunning," he murmured, working hard to draw a breath into his lungs. "Absolutely stunning."

She smiled nervously. "Why, thank you, Mr. Cooper, you don't look so bad yourself."

Dex glanced down at his white shirt, black tie and jeans. Pretty simple, really. But the best he could do considering Ty was no clothes horse.

"Thank you, ma'am," he drawled, then offered his arm. "Shall we go?"

He walked her to the passenger side of the truck and opened the door. "Wait, I almost forgot something," he said as he reached inside. He withdrew the small box and offered it to her.

"What's this?" she asked, breathless.

"Open it," he urged. "You'll see."

Her hands shaking with impatience she quickly loosened the ribbon and removed the lid. "Oh, it's beautiful." She took the blue and white carnation wrist corsage from the box and smiled up at him, her eyes suspiciously bright. "Thank you, Ty. That was very sweet of you."

He slipped it onto her right wrist. "Can't take a lady to a dance without a corsage." He smiled, warmth filling his chest, reminding him of how sweet this particular lady was.

She pressed a quick kiss to his cheek, then shook her head. "I swear, Ty, it's like I don't even know you anymore."

He held out his hand to assist her into the vehicle. "Are you saying I'm not always this nice?"

"No, it's not that." She adjusted her dress, then looked at him. "But you took my idea of opening a dude ranch far better than I could have hoped." She lifted one slender shoulder in the barest of shrugs. "Now flowers." She reached up and felt his forehead. "It makes me wonder if you've come down with something."

What did Ty have against her opening a dude ranch? he wondered. Could he have overstepped his bounds there? They would have to discuss that as soon as Dex had a chance to call him, which had better be soon.

He gifted Leanne with a smile. "I've just decided that life's too short to sweat the small stuff. There's always a way to work anything out," he assured her, hoping like hell he was right.

When they arrived at the Rolling Bend community center the place was already packed. The band was loud, as Grandmother Cooper had said it would be, and the night was warm. Dex escorted Leanne to the door, but she stopped him when he would have opened it.

"Ty." She looked up at him, those pretty blue eyes far too serious. "Just for tonight could we pretend that we're not who we are?"

Confused, Dex tried to read her expression for some hint of what she was thinking. "I don't know what you mean."

She placed a soft hand on his arm, sending heat rushing through him. "Just for tonight, let's pretend you're not Ty Cooper, the rancher who loves nothing more than raising his cattle. That I'm not Leanne Watley, struggling dude rancher. And that our parents haven't tried to marry us off for years. Let's just be two people who want to have a nice time together for one evening. Just one night," she added softly.

The urge to take her in his arms and show her just what they could do together if they forgot for this one night was almost more than he could restrain.

"We can do that." He stared directly into her eyes, hunger roaring inside him. At that moment he would have given anything to *really* have her for one night. "Just for tonight."

He opened the door and they entered the loud, exuberant festivities. He wondered if Miss Leanne

Watley had any idea how close to the edge she'd pushed him. It would take nothing short of a miracle to keep him from crossing the line tonight.

BEFORE Ty could have the first dance with her, Leanne found herself whirled around the dance floor with half a dozen different young men. All single, all hoping she was looking for a husband. Did people around here think of nothing else?

Her gaze sought and found Ty. He looked so handsome. He'd abandoned his hat, leaving it on their table, but he looked even better without it. Why had she never noticed that before? She wanted desperately to run her fingers through that thick, dark hair. All week this crazy attraction had been building. She just couldn't get him off her mind. Finally, she'd decided there was only one way. She closed her eyes and wished they could really be together in the truest sense of the word for just this one night. Maybe she would realize it was nothing but raging hormones.

But Ty was too honorable for that. If they made love, especially under the circumstances, he would demand that they marry.

Sometimes being a virgin could be so annoying.

Ty looked up from his conversation with Mr. Dickson from the hardware. His gaze caught hers and he smiled. Her heart did that little acrobatic flip only he had the power to cause. The song ended and her dance partner thanked her. She wove her way around the fringes of the crowd. A fast, bluegrass tune started and the dancers still on the floor kicked their heels high and let go whoops of enthusiasm.

Earlier, Jenny Cooper had announced that she and

Chad were expecting. Angelica, their little girl, looked downright miserable. Leanne was happy for Jenny and Chad, but she couldn't quite work up the proper enthusiasm. She told herself she wasn't jealous. She didn't even want to get married.

But part of her did, she admitted glumly, then chastised herself. Where on earth had that thought come from? She tried to understand it, rationalize it somehow, but she couldn't. It simply was. She *wanted* to be Mrs. Ty Cooper. Part of her wanted to have his babies. She shook her head and reached for a cup of punch. But a saner part of her wanted to do just what she was doing. None of this should be happening. It didn't make sense. Lord have mercy, she'd never been this confused in her life.

A wide palm settled against the small of her back and a familiar body, warm and muscular, moved in close to hers. "May I have this dance, pretty lady?"

Leanne sat her cup down and looked up into Ty's dark eyes. "I thought you'd never ask."

He smiled. Her heart flip-flopped. "I was waiting for the perfect moment."

Only then did she realize that a slow, aching love song had started to play. He led her to the dance floor, then drew her into his arms. As those strong arms closed around her, pulling her against the shelter of his lean body, everything else faded away. She inhaled the masculine scents of leather and spice, looked up into a face she knew as well as her own. But when she closed her eyes and laid her head against him, it was as if he were someone else.

She had danced with Ty many times before, but this time was different. The way he held her...the perfect rhythm of his movements…the feel of his hands as he traced her spine. The feel of his lips against her forehead. Her heart raced with anticipation, her pulse throbbed impatiently. This couldn't be real, she assured herself, but she clung to the moment with both hands. She wanted this one moment. Her fingers found their way into his hair. He reacted, pressing her more firmly against his hips, allowing her to feel how she moved him.

One song melded into another. It was as if the band knew they didn't want to part, so the slow, sensual music continued. She could feel the steady beating of his heart beneath her cheek, could feel each defined muscle of his lean body. She wanted to rip his shirt open and touch all that skin she'd seen the other day in her kitchen. She wanted him to kiss her again.

God, she wanted him to kiss her again.

Reacting on instinct, she turned her face up to his. A new rush of need flooded her when she saw her own desire mirrored in his eyes. He wanted her, too. Wanted her just as much as she wanted him. She could feel his breath on her skin, but he made no move to do what she wanted so badly.

She lifted her chin, putting her lips so close to his, close enough to feel the electricity sizzle between them. She felt his exhalation of frustration. He was holding back and she didn't want to hold back, not tonight. Tonight nothing else was supposed to matter. She stilled, then tiptoed, making the contact complete. He released her instantly, his hands going immediately to cup her face.

His mouth claimed hers with a gentle fierceness that made her knees go weak. On and on he caressed her lips with his own, tasting, teasing. Then he sealed his lips over hers completely, the move rougher, more frantic. This was the moment she'd waited for, she realized, as foolish as it was. His hot tongue thrust into her mouth. She whimpered, pulling him closer. His fingers threaded into her hair, angling her head to give him better access. His tongue glided along hers, sending fire straight to her center, then touched her so intimately, her feminine muscles clenched in response.

He drew back, his ragged breath fanning her sizzling lips. "If I don't stop now, I may not be able to," he murmured thickly.

She nodded, speech was impossible. They were no longer dancing, only holding each other in such an intimate embrace that it was impossible not to see the heat simmering between them. But she didn't care. She wanted this night. She wanted more. She wanted it now.

"Can we please leave?"

He looked startled.

"Please," she urged.

He searched her eyes for ten full seconds. She struggled not to show any doubt. This was what she wanted. Now.

He grabbed her hand and cut a path through the crowd, pulling her along behind him, and snagging his hat as they went. She focused her gaze on his broad shoulders rather than on the couples stopping to stare at them. She no longer cared what anyone thought. She simply wanted.

She wanted this man.

Tonight.

And for the first time in her life she was going to take what she wanted with no thought to the consequences.

He kept walking. He didn't stop until he reached the driver's side of his truck. Far enough, she decided when he would have reached for the door. She pulled him around to face her, the heat in those dark eyes searing her.

"Kiss me again," she demanded, feeling even bolder.

He did. Drew her hard against him, the fingers of one hand kneading her buttocks, lifting her into him. This was no sweet, tender kiss. This was rough and hot, almost frightening.

He turned her loose long enough to open the door. She climbed in at his ushering and scooted across the bench seat, he slid in next to her, shoving his hat onto the dash.

"Where are we going?" he asked, his voice as rough as his kiss, the sound making her shiver.

"I don't care." She leaned toward him and kissed his mouth again. "Anywhere."

He started the engine and spun out of the parking lot. Leanne's heart was pounding so hard she could scarcely draw a breath. Please don't let him change his mind, she prayed. She knew Ty too well. If he thought about it…if she really thought about it.

No.

She had to do something to keep up the momentum. But what? She had no experience with this kind of situation. But she had seen lots of movies. She scooted closer to him. He smiled at her, the expression strained.

Oh yes, she had to do something or he was going to change his mind. She loosened the string tie and tugged it from his collar. He accelerated as if that simple move had somehow urged him on. Feeling empowered, she unfastened the button at his collar. His fingers tightened on the steering wheel. She smiled. This was really something. She opened another button, then another. With each move his breathing become more labored and a muscle flexed in his chiseled jaw. It was working, not to mention driving her wild.

She reached inside his shirt and touched him. She gasped at the feel of his skin. His right arm went around her and drew her closer. He pressed a kiss to her temple. She was breathing so hard and fast she felt lightheaded. She couldn't believe the way it made her feel just to touch his skin. It was so smooth, so hot. She wanted more. Another button, then another. Then she leaned between him and the steering wheel and tasted that amazing terrain.

He groaned, the sound savage, like an animal. She could hear him breathing...or was it her? Her lips brushed one flat male nipple. The fingers of his right hand fisted in her hair, telegraphing his approval of that move. She did it again, this time she lingered, touched it with the tip of her tongue. He made more sounds. She sucked. He swore. While she tortured that nipple, her palm slid instinctively down his flat belly. She tugged at his belt, then fumbled with the fly of his jeans.

He made a hard right, pulling the truck onto a side road, then ramming the gear shift into Park. The engine died. The lights went out and his hands were all over her at once.

He slid to the middle of the bench seat and pulled her astride his hips. He lowered her mouth to his and kissed her so hard it almost hurt. Her hands continued to explore his chest, teasing his nipples the way he liked, and molding to each contour of male muscle.

He tugged one thin strap from her shoulder, then lowered the bodice of her dress just far enough to expose one breast. For one long moment he only stared at the small, pale globe, his breathing so harsh the sound made her ache in a way she'd never known before. When his mouth closed over her breast, she screamed her pleasure. His hips rose from the seat, thrusting against her. She pushed down, reveling in the hard feel of him against the place that ached so for his touch.

Then he suddenly stopped. She moaned her displeasure. She didn't want him to stop.

"I can't do this." His words were barely audible above his ragged breathing.

"Please don't stop." She kissed his lips in hopes of changing his mind, at the same time pressing down against him. He groaned.

"Wait." He held her away from him and looked at her in the darkness. She could just make out his eyes, the grim set of his mouth. "We can't."

"I don't understand." She shook her head. "Don't you want me?"

"Oh, yes." He gently lifted her off him and settled her on the seat beside him. "But we can't do this." He shook his head. "It wouldn't be right for either of us."

She dropped her head back against the seat. "I can't believe this."

He slid behind the wheel once more and started the engine. "Neither can I."

He drove her home without another word.

Chapter Nine

By the time Ty parked in front of her house Leanne was feeling more than a little embarrassed. What in the world had possessed her to behave so foolishly? Ty probably thought she'd lost her mind. She stole a glance at him. But he'd been a little out of control, too. She closed her eyes and shook her head. The truth was she'd pushed him into it. What man wouldn't react willingly with a woman practically taking advantage of him? She thought of that muscled, masculine frame, then of her own size and decided maybe *taking advantage* was a bit of an overstatement.

She'd just wanted this one night.

Just to see. To get this crazy thing settled once and for all. Then things could return to normal, she felt sure.

Without looking at her, Ty got out of the truck and walked around to her door to see her out. When he opened it, she looked at him in the dim glow cast by the cab light. She saw the same confusion she felt and something else...regret?

Her heart sank, adding insult to injury. She slipped

off the seat to stand directly in front of him. To her surprise he made no move to back away. He just waited. For her to say something, she supposed.

"I'm sorry," she said in a braver tone than she'd thought possible. "I don't know what came over me." She trembled but quickly crossed her arms over her chest to conceal the quaking.

He touched her cheek, those long fingers trailed along her jawline, making her shiver, before he dropped his hand back to his side. "You have nothing to be sorry for," he assured her, his voice as soft and gentle as his touch. "We both got a little carried away tonight." He smiled; her heart reacted. "The pressure has been on both of us and maybe we just needed to see what all the fuss was about."

He didn't sound convinced but his effort to make her feel better touched her. "Thanks, Ty." She peered up at him, once more amazed at how she could have known him all this time and not realized just how wonderful he was. "You're a good sport and I'm…" She shrugged. "I think I'm just confused."

"Let's forget about it, okay?" He ushered her away from the truck door so that he could close it, then toward her porch steps, his palm never leaving the small of her back.

Forget it. That was the way he handled everything lately. A jab of anger made her want to stop right there and tell him what she thought. It sure hadn't felt like he wanted to forget it when they were kissing. He'd been very aroused. She might not have any experience with men, but she knew when one was aroused. She'd read her share of romance novels and watched enough romantic movies. And now he wanted to act as if it had been nothing. This whole situation bordered on the ridiculous. All this time they'd been friends, now suddenly everything was spiraling out of control, and he wanted to pretend it all away.

Why couldn't she do the same? That was the truly frustrating part.

Leanne squared her shoulders and lifted her chin in defiance of her own doubts. Whatever was going on with her foolish heart, she'd get over it. Ty was right, they should simply forget the whole thing.

At her door, she turned back to him, head held high. "Good night, Ty. Thank you for taking me to the dance."

He moistened those full lips, causing a little hitch in her breathing. She swore silently. He appeared more uncertain now of what had happened than she did. He quickly, awkwardly pressed a chaste kiss to her cheek, lingering just long enough for her to be assaulted all over again by that tantalizing masculine scent.

"Good night," he murmured.

Leanne turned away from him, gave the doorknob a frantic twist and rushed into her living room. The urge to cry was nearly overwhelming. This was insane! Her emotions were on a roller-coaster ride. One minute she wanted to push him away, the next—

"Leanne?"

The weak sound of her mother's voice came from somewhere in the dark living room. "Mom?"

"I can't seem to get up."

Panic shot through Leanne. She felt for the light switch and snapped it on. Her mother lay in a crumpled heap on the floor, struggling hard to raise herself to a sitting position. "Mom!" Leanne rushed to her side. "Are you hurt?" Fear made her heart pound. She should have been at home tonight, not out misbehaving as she had. Guilt and worry swamped her. She should never have left her mother at home alone for so long.

"Is everything all right?"

When Leanne looked up Ty was striding into the room, concern marring his handsome face. He crouched next to her. "What happened?"

"She fell. Help me get her to her bed."

As Leanne tried to help her mother up, he halted her with a firm hand on her shoulder. "Wait. We can't move her yet." He eased closer to her mother, effectively nudging Leanne out of the way. "Mrs. Watley, are you in pain? Did you hurt yourself when you fell?"

Leanne's worry deepened into a frown as she watched him. He was examining her mother, checking her limbs, turning her head from side-to-side. A new surge of concern washed over her. What if her mother had broken something? A hip or her arm? Lord, she should have been here.

"No," her mother told him. "I don't think I'm hurt. Just gave myself a good fright." She smiled weakly. "Then I didn't have the strength to get up. But I'll be fine. I just need to get back to my room, that's all. I shouldn't have come downstairs without help."

Ty looked doubtful. He helped her mother into a sitting position, then studied her eyes. "Did you hit your head? Is your vision blurred? Do you feel dizzy or lightheaded?''

"I didn't hit my head, and I can see fine.'' Joanna patted Ty's arm. "Really. I'm fine. There's no need to fret so.''

He assisted her to her feet while Leanne stood helplessly by, feeling like an outsider in her own home. "Let me help you to your room,'' she said quickly as Ty was about to speak again. She slid one arm around her mother's waist and led her slowly toward the staircase.

"I'm fine, really,'' her mother insisted. "I can manage. You should see to your company.''

Leanne glanced over her shoulder at Ty, who appeared deep in thought as he watched their slow progress. "Ty'll be fine for a few minutes while I help you to your room.''

"Take your time,'' he said, his tone somehow strained.

When Leanne had her mother safely back in bed, she asked, "Can I get you anything? Water? Milk?'' Her mother shook her head. She looked so frail, so weary. Leanne wanted to cry. It just wasn't fair for her mother to suffer this way. Leanne sat down on her bedside. "I'm sorry I left you here alone,'' she murmured. "I shouldn't have.''

Her mother reached up and stroked her cheek, affection shining in her eyes. "Don't be silly, child. I wanted you to go. I would have been fine if I hadn't gotten up to sit on the couch and wait for you.'' She shook her head. "It was foolish, but I wanted to be waiting for you when you got home like I used to do.''

Leanne kissed her forehead, trying hard to restrain the tears burning in her eyes. "You rest now. I'll tell you all about the dance in the morning."

Her mother patted her hand. "You go on back down there and see to Ty. I think he's a little upset. I hope I didn't ruin your evening."

The concern in her eyes tugged at Leanne's heartstrings. She forced a smile. "'Course you didn't." She stood. "Good night, Mama."

"Night." Her mother closed her eyes and seemed to drift immediately to sleep.

Leanne watched a few moments longer just to be sure her mother was resting. As she left the room she turned out the light, then closed the door. She pressed her forehead against the cool wooden surface and fought the urge to weep. If only there was something she could do to make her mother well again. If she could just talk her into seeing that specialist Dr. Baker had suggested. But Joanna Watley could be as stubborn as a mule at times. She would not go to a specialist. Leanne knew it was the money and she hated the idea that her mother was suffering because Leanne couldn't work more quickly. Couldn't make things happen at a faster rate.

Another reason she should marry Ty. She shivered at the memory of how it felt to be in his arms. He'd made her heart flip-flop just like she'd known the only one for her would. She stilled. But she didn't love him...not like that, did she? And he hadn't wanted to make love to her. He'd stopped, called it a mistake.

Leanne sighed. God, she was hopeless. How could she have all these tangled feelings? This sudden attraction was most likely temporary. Maybe it was about sex. Maybe she'd simply outgrown her virginity. Maybe that was the whole problem.

She composed herself and headed back down to the living room where Ty waited. That was it, she decided. This whole crazy week had been about nothing but hormones. It was a simple biological urge. It had nothing to do with love or Ty. He was just handy.

One look at the man waiting in her living room made a liar out of her where that last thought was concerned. The man standing there, his shirt wrinkled by her frantic hands, that thick, dark hair mussed by her urgent fingers, was more than just handy. He was good-looking, sexy and he made her tingle low in her belly. He made her want to finish what they'd started.

Those dark eyes connected with hers and the fierceness there brought her up short. "Tell me about your mother's health."

It wasn't a request. Leanne felt oddly off balance by the harsh demand. "It started last year." She frowned as she considered the question. "You know that. It seems to have gotten worse over the past couple of months. Doc—"

"What exactly is *it?*" Another demand. "There must be a diagnosis."

Leanne swallowed back the hurt that accompanied what she recognized as accusation in his eyes. "Dr. Baker isn't exactly sure. He's ruled out lupus and rheumatoid arthritis, but—"

"Has she seen an internist?"

"A what?"

Ty took a breath, clearly to slow his temper. He was angry. She could see it in his eyes, his posture. This didn't make sense.

"This Dr. Baker, he hasn't referred her to anyone else or requested any other specialized testing? There are literally hundreds of different tests that her symptoms might indicate."

Defensive now, Leanne crossed her arms over her chest and glared at him. She was too annoyed to care how he could know so much about medicine and suddenly seem to have forgotten all he'd known about her mother's illness. "Well, of course he has. You know how thorough Dr. Baker is. But she refuses to see anyone else. She thinks we can't afford a specialist. It—"

There was no mistaking the fury in those dark eyes now. "Money again?" he snapped. A muscle jumped in his tense jaw. "Did it never occur to you to simply ask for help? Your mother is ill. Not having the strength to pick herself up from the floor is not likely to be some simple, passing ailment that will go away by itself. She needs the proper treatment." He stepped nearer, that fierce gaze boring down on her. "But before she can get that, she has to have the proper diagnosis. There's no excuse for lack of appropriate health care."

He was accusing Leanne of failing somehow. "What do you think I've been doing? I've tried everything I know to make her go, but she won't. She thinks we can't afford it and she's right, but I can't convince her to go and that we'll make it somehow."

"She's your mother," he all but growled. "You shouldn't take no for an answer."

His words stabbed her like a knife. Maybe he was right. Maybe she hadn't taken a firm enough stand on the issue. But she had so much on her. The ranch.

Taking care of everything. Finding a way to make every penny stretch as far as possible. Getting the guest cabins ready. A fresh wave of tears welled. But maybe it was her fault.

"I've done the best I could considering—"

"Obviously," he cut her off, "it hasn't been enough. You'll call her doctor first thing in the morning," he said sharply.

She could only nod. How could he think she didn't care? How could he believe she'd been negligent?

"Good," he said with a bit less ferocity, then looked away and took another of those deep breaths that did nothing to calm the outrage clear in his rigid posture. "I should go."

Leanne felt empty, hurt and too confused to know exactly why he'd lashed out at her this way or why it should wound her so deeply. "I'd like you to go."

He swallowed, hard, then started to say something else, but apparently changed his mind.

He walked out.

She locked the door behind him.

Taking a deep, bolstering breath she trudged across the room and sat down on the edge of the couch, suddenly exhausted. She stared down at the silky blue fabric puddled around her feet and thought of how Ty had wanted her to have this dress. She thought about how he'd kissed her…how he'd touched her…

And then she cried.

Cried for reasons she didn't even understand.

Cried so hard that her chest hurt.

Or maybe it was her heart. She wasn't sure she would ever be the same again.

HE'D DRIVEN AROUND for hours. Hell, he'd even gotten lost once. But he just couldn't go home.

Home?

Dex laughed, a humorless sound. The Circle C wasn't his home, no matter how much it felt like home when he finally parked between the house and barn around 1:00 a.m. He stared at the big old farmhouse, noting that the front porch light had been left on, for him.

He'd never felt so disgusted or confused in his entire life. He got out of the truck and walked to the porch, his feet leaden, his chest even heavier. He'd been a real bastard tonight. Though he would never understand why anyone would allow their health problems to go unmonitored when good medical care was certainly available, even in the wilds of Montana, he shouldn't have taken his fury out on Leanne.

She hadn't deserved it.

But the idea that she would go along with her mother was simply beyond his comprehension.

Still not ready to go inside, Dex collapsed onto the porch swing. He'd hurt her. There was no way he could have missed the pain in her eyes or in her voice when she'd told him to go. She was so young and innocent, and he was such a fool.

"Idiot," he muttered. He leaned forward, braced his elbows on his knees and tunneled his fingers through his hair. He had absolutely no experience where these sorts of affairs were concerned. Briefly he wondered where he'd left Ty's hat. In the truck, he decided, trying to focus on **anything** else. But the echo of his own words kept replaying in his head, overriding all other thought. He was a complete fool.

How could he have spoken to her like that? Now he'd have to find some way to make this up to her, to bring that smile back to her lips.

The thought of her lips made his stomach tighten as he pictured every moment they'd shared tonight. Her eager kisses. The way she'd begged him not to stop. He'd wanted her more than he'd ever wanted any woman in his life.

But he couldn't do this. He would be leaving soon and he didn't want to hurt her. Besides, the whole town appeared to want Leanne and Ty to spend the rest of their lives together. Dex couldn't do anything to mess that up. For all he knew Ty was simply suffering from cold feet and might want Leanne when he returned. Dex couldn't risk hurting her or his brother.

He leaned back in the swing and shook his head. What a mess. He'd royally screwed up at every step. He couldn't understand or justify all the mixed-up emotions he felt. In Atlanta he made life-altering decisions every day regarding patient care, research, personnel. How could he feel so differently, so emotionally disabled here?

It just didn't make sense.

He closed his eyes and thought about the way Jenny had hugged him earlier tonight. She was so excited to learn that she was pregnant. Why had her news affected him on the level it had? He'd felt something, something he couldn't name. A fondness, pride. He shook his head. Something. Even Angelica and the twins had gotten to him.

Lady sauntered over to the swing, her tail wagging, then plopped down near his feet. He'd passed the final test, he mused, the family dog had grown to like him. Did all this mean he was a part of the Cooper family now?

He shook his head again. None of it counted. They all thought he was Ty. They would all be confused and hurt when it was over. Whatever had possessed him to believe that anything could be gained by this ruse?

Feeling too damned confused, he tugged out his wallet and removed the picture of his parents. He stared at the smiling couple in the photograph. They looked so happy, each holding a tiny bundle. Dex had no way of knowing which was him and which was Ty.

Why did his parents have to die?

Dex blinked back the uncharacteristic sting of tears. He was thirty-two years old. He was a doctor, for Christ's sake. He wasn't supposed to ask foolish questions like that.

The squeak of the screen door dragged him from his painful reverie. Grandmother Cooper, clad in a pale pink robe and matching fuzzy house slippers shuffled across the porch in his direction. This was the first time he'd seen her with her hair down. A long gray braid draped one shoulder. She smiled that smile that made him feel serene somehow.

"My, you did have a late night, didn't you, son?" She sat down beside him, her gaze going directly to the photograph in his hand.

Dex almost groaned. He'd forgotten about the picture. Now she would know. He returned her smile. "Yeah, I guess I did have a long night."

She nodded at the photograph in his hand. "I wondered where that picture had gotten to."

Surprised, Dex studied her for a long moment. "You knew it was missing?"

She leaned back against the polished wood slats, her gaze taking on a distant look. "There isn't a day goes by that I don't look at each and every one of those pictures."

It was difficult to breathe. Dex blinked at the emotion burning in his eyes yet again. He wanted desperately to know more, to ask her all the questions that twisted inside him. "You still miss them?" The one question was barely a whisper, but it brought another smile to her lips.

"More now than ever."

He needed so many answers but he couldn't bring himself to ask another single question. Rather, he nodded his head once in silent agreement.

She hugged him, then. Hugged him fiercely. The gentle fragrance of lilacs filled his nostrils. He closed his eyes and allowed himself to relax into the embrace of the woman who'd given birth to his mother. The woman whose smile opened a window to a past he hadn't known existed.

"I'm so glad you're home," she murmured. "I've missed you."

He was touched deeply and at the same time startled by her words. Sensing his tension, she drew back and pointed to the picture he still clutched in his hand.

"In that moment, your mother and father were the happiest of their entire lives. They were complete with each other." She leveled him with a watery gaze that left no question as to what she meant. "And with you and your brother."

A frown tugged at Dex's brow. He started to ask the one question that burned in his chest, but she spoke again before he could get the words out past the lump in his throat.

"It wasn't enough that we lost your mother and father, we had to lose one of the babies, too." Her gaze grew distant again, her tone wistful. "It was the hardest thing I've ever endured." She looked back at him. "But don't doubt for a second how much we loved you both." She placed a hand on his arm and squeezed gently. "We never stopped loving *both of you.*"

She kissed his cheek, got up and went back into the house.

Dex watched her, too moved or too stunned to speak.

He looked down at the picture in his hand once more and thought of the things his grandmother had just said to him and suddenly he knew.

He scrubbed a hand across his damp face as a strained laugh burst out of him.

He wasn't sure how it could be possible, but he was relatively certain of one thing: she knew.

Grandmother Cooper knew his secret.

Chapter Ten

By Monday morning Dex was certain he had things back under control. Despite what had happened between them on Friday night, he'd shown up at Leanne's house on Saturday morning, business as usual. He was dependable if nothing else. When a Montgomery gave his word, he didn't go back on it.

Staring at his reflection in the mirror, Dex fastened the last button of his shirt and finger-combed his hair. As one would suspect, things had been a little tense with Leanne. He felt like the jerk he was for being so hard on her about her mother. It was clear that she loved her and had done the best she could. She certainly couldn't force her to seek out additional medical attention.

In his heart he knew that Leanne had gone above and beyond her duty as a daughter. As far as he could tell she had no life outside of taking care of her mother and the ranch. He felt like kicking himself. As a physician, sometimes he failed to see that things weren't always black and white. Sometimes there were extenuating circumstances beyond one's control. He'd started to explain himself on several occasions, but she always changed the subject or insisted she had to go check on something. Finally, he'd given up.

Making amends wasn't his specialty. Besides, she seemed satisfied with leaving things the way they were. Why rock the boat? They had definitely needed something to extinguish the fire building between them. It was best for all concerned.

Neither of them needed that kind of complication.

He'd even spent Sunday afternoon at Leanne's. He'd had to do something to escape the family's scrutiny. It wasn't enough that he'd attended church services with the whole clan on Sunday morning and then endured endless matchmaking hints and suggestions during lunch—which the Coopers called dinner. Grandfather Cooper had suggested that after the meal of fried chicken, homemade rolls, peas, mashed potatoes and gravy, he and Dex should have a man-to-man talk about women and marriage.

Dex'd had no choice. He had to find a way to escape. Spending the afternoon *not talking* to Leanne while they painted yet another of the cabins was preferable to the "talk." If he could live through the fire-and-brimstone sermon the minister had delivered, Dex decided, he could do anything. Several times during the discourse he'd felt certain the man was speaking to him personally, but that was impossible. Wasn't it?

A wistful feeling surged through Dex. He did miss his family. In spite of everything, he wondered how the Montgomerys were doing and if Ty had been accepted by them as he had been here.

Very soon he had to find a private moment to call Ty and find out how it was going in Atlanta. With a family this size it was almost impossible to find a second alone near the one telephone in the house. At this point he wasn't too worried. He assumed that since Ty had not made any frantic calls to him, all must be well.

Dex picked up his hat and slowly turned it in his hands as he considered that late-night conversation on the porch with his grandmother. He couldn't be absolutely certain, but he had a feeling she knew. His stomach tied up in knots every time he thought about how she'd hugged him and told him she'd always loved both of them, and that she was glad he was home. He ran an unsteady hand through his hair and swallowed with difficulty. Would all the Coopers be so accepting? Especially when they discovered that he'd lied to them, misled them for his own benefit?

The image of Leanne filled his mind. How would she feel? He sighed, anxiety nagging at him. He didn't want her to be hurt by any of this. Watching her this weekend, especially yesterday, had kept him breathless.

There was something about the fit of her jeans and the worn T-shirt that made her look vulnerable yet so seductive. His throat had gone dry every time their eyes met, but she'd turned away from him each time. She hadn't wanted to look him in the eye. And it was all his fault.

Now, the next day, Dex stared at the floor; even he was unable to look himself in the eye in the mirror. Life wasn't fair sometimes. He'd had everything he ever wanted. Leanne worked so hard, and yet she and her mother went without more often than not and were too proud to ask for help or even accept what was offered.

The inner strength of the people he'd met here amazed him. Would he be able to face such adversity so well? A frown inched across his brow. He didn't know. He'd never been faced with these kinds of sacrifices.

Dex squared his shoulders and glared at his reflection. He'd always been a man of action. There was no reason he couldn't be one now. Dex Montgomery wasn't down for the count just yet. He knew people, had connections. He could get things done that no one else could. The circumstances definitely called for action. Leanne's mother needed a specialist. Fine. He could take care of that. Ensuring that the dude ranch got off to a good start would be a simple matter as well. He'd find a way to see that she succeeded. The Coopers needed to improve the Circle C's cattle market. He could help with that, too. The first thing one did when seeking out new clients was to give off an appearance of quality and efficiency. Appearances were everything. Organization was the key.

And there was no better organizer on the planet than Dex Montgomery.

Thirty minutes later Dex met with Chad and Court outside the main barn.

"I want every single asset inventoried," he told the two men staring agog at him. "I've noticed that our two ranch hands aren't always occupied. I want the barns, the storage buildings and the equipment sheds reorganized ASAP." He handed Court the quick instructions he'd jotted down. "That should get them started. Feel free to add to or change the organization layout as necessary.''

''But we've had things the same way for years,'' Chad protested, still looking a little startled by the orders.

Dex gave him an understanding pat on the back. ''The future is about change, bro. The only businesses moving into the future are the ones willing to allow change.'' He gave the younger man a conspiratorial wink. ''The Coopers are about to move into the twenty-first century.''

With his instructions relayed, Dex headed back to the house. He wanted to take a quick look at the book-keeping process and see how Ty and his grandfather handled that end of things. He would still make it to Leanne's that afternoon. They had almost finished the cabins anyway. But he had to find a way to get the cabins furnished without her going postal on him.

Dex paused in the kitchen long enough to pour himself a cup of coffee. He closed his eyes and enjoyed the full-flavored taste of Grandmother Cooper's own special blend. The woman knew how to mix her coffee beans. Decaffeinated or not, it was the best he'd ever had.

''I hear you're raising quite a ruckus with your brothers.''

Dex opened his eyes and instantly smiled at his grandmother. She'd obviously been outside and overheard their conversation. The twinkle in her eyes told him that she wasn't bothered by his sudden attitude change.

''Sometimes things need to change,'' he offered,

his words carrying a hidden meaning she would understand if, as he suspected, she knew.

She nodded, her gaze a bit more guarded now. "That's true enough."

He angled his head in the direction of the large walk-in pantry and grinned. "I couldn't help but notice that the pantry could use a little reorganizing as well."

She arched an eyebrow. "Don't even think about it," she warned. "The womenfolk will take care of the house."

His coffee in hand, still grinning from ear to ear, Dex sauntered into the downstairs room just off the family room that served as the office. His grandfather was busy at the calculator. Dex sat down at the other desk, the one Ty used, and started going through the files. His grandfather merely glanced at him over his bifocals, his fingers never letting up on the keypad.

Within a couple of hours Dex had a pretty good handle on the Coopers' finances. They had a good solid portfolio. Not great, but definitely good. He saw room for improvement in several areas.

Grandfather Cooper stood and stretched. "Well, I think I've done all the damage I can this morning." He scratched his chest. "Maybe I'll just go see if that heavenly smell coming from the kitchen is cookies."

Frowning, Dex looked up from his notes. He'd spent the last twenty or so minutes looking at ways to expand, or, at the very least, increase profits.

"One question," he said, before the older man could leave the room.

His grandfather turned back, his face expectant.

"Why is it we've never charged the bordering

McCaleb ranch for water rights? The river is clearly on Cooper land which they have to cross to reach it.'' He pointed to the aerial photograph on the wall. ''I'm quite certain that could be an additional source of revenue.''

The older man's expression darkened. He strode over to where Dex sat and stared hard down at him. ''Young man, I don't know what high-faluting ideas they put in your head in Chicago at that investors' meeting, but I can tell you one thing right now, we don't do business that way around here.''

Surprised at his outrage, Dex flared his hands. ''I'm only suggesting—''

''I know what you're suggesting,'' he said, cutting Dex off. His grandfather eased one hip onto the edge of the desk and visibly struggled for calm. ''The McCalebs are our neighbors. You don't charge neighbors when they share in the blessings you're fortunate enough to receive.'' When Dex would have offered an alternative perspective, Grandfather Cooper held up a hand, halting the interruption. ''We've always helped our neighbors, son. That won't change in the future, investors or no investors. Furthermore, they've always helped us whenever we needed an extra hand. No suggestion from some fancy, shmancy restaurant chain is going to better what the Lord intended the day he handed down the law to Moses.''

He'd lost Dex completely, but he tried not to show it.

''When the good Lord said to do unto others as you'd have them do unto you, he meant it.'' Grandfather Cooper pushed off the desk and clapped Dex on the back. ''That includes neighbors. Don't you go forgetting the golden rule, boy. There's nothing in this life more important. Nothing.''

Dex sat thinking for a long while after his grandfather had gone. *Golden rule.* Now he knew the one indisputable difference between the Coopers and the Montgomerys. The Montgomerys wanted to succeed. At all costs. The Coopers wanted to succeed in their business as well, except that they wanted everyone around them to succeed, too. Dex shook his head. It didn't make sense. In today's cutthroat marketplace it didn't pay to bleed when your neighbor was cut. But the Coopers did.

It went against every deeply ingrained business tactic Dex had ever been taught.

Maybe he'd been wrong about what the Coopers needed. All the reorganization in the world couldn't replace heart.

A new respect sprouted inside Dex. Hard work was what kept these people surviving one generation after the next, regardless of the obstacles life threw in their way.

Heart was what made them who they were.

An idea formed on the heels of that epiphany. There were lots of things one could do under the umbrella of being *neighborly.* Dex grinned. Lots and lots of things.

LEANNE TRUDGED up the back steps just as it was getting dark on Friday evening. She'd never been so tired in her whole life. At least all the painting was finished. She had Ty to thank for that. She paused on the top step and sat down to rest for a few moments.

Things had been strained between them all week.

Not really unpleasant, just tense. He was careful what he said to her, she was careful what she said to him. They tiptoed around each other, not wanting to touch accidentally. As good as his word, he'd shown up every single day and worked hard to help her finish. Next week she would be ready to visit the bank president about a start-up loan. She'd keep the furnishings simple for the time being, and she could put the pool start-up costs off until she actually had bookings. She felt confident for the first time in a long time that she could actually do this. And she owed it all to Ty.

She'd never have gotten this far this quickly without his generosity. She still couldn't figure out why he'd gone along with her plan so easily. The fact of the matter was, there seemed to be a lot of things she couldn't quite figure out about him lately, not the least of which was this considerable attraction brewing between them.

She'd known Ty her entire life and now it was as if he was a stranger. He hadn't been the same since he returned from Chicago. She'd struggled the whole time he was gone to try and work up the courage to tell him about the dude ranch, had even offered to pick him up at the airport to give them some time alone together. But she'd lost her nerve, not to mention she'd been disconcerted by his peculiar behavior.

Strange behavior that entailed far more than this wild attraction between them. It was in everything he did and said—how he handled himself. His walk was even different. His touch. The way he looked at her. Maybe Angelica was right, maybe Ty had been taken over by aliens. Leanne smiled at the idea. She and Jenny had laughed until they both cried at the little girl's accusation. Leanne's smile faded as she considered the concept further. What if Angelica was simply noticing the same things Leanne had noticed…that Ty wasn't the same. Not the same at all.

She'd seen movies where people suddenly started to behave in bizarre manners, it usually involved drugs or some life-altering event. She frowned. But nothing like that had happened to Ty. She shrugged and pushed to her feet. Maybe it was just the strain of trying to venture into new markets. Maybe that's why he hadn't fussed when Leanne told him what she wanted to do.

She paused again at the door and allowed that now-familiar warmth to sear through her as she thought of the way it had felt to be held in his arms…to be kissed by him. It was magical and totally surprising. Who would've thought that she'd be feeling this way? She shook her head. Silly girl, she chastised. Ty had made it clear this week that he'd wanted to keep his distance. She should follow his example. Attraction wasn't enough. She wanted to be head over heels in love and she wasn't there.

She swallowed tightly.

Not yet anyway.

She opened the kitchen door and went inside. A long hot bath was what she needed now, not sinful thoughts of Ty Cooper.

A decidedly feminine and definitely unfamiliar voice stopped Leanne in her tracks. She froze, listening. Then she heard her mother's frail voice. Leanne relaxed. They apparently had company. Taking a breath, she headed for the living room to see who'd stopped by. They rarely had guests.

She was startled to find a woman, in her thirties maybe, dressed in a professional business suit, putting a bandage in the bend of her mother's elbow. Leanne stared at her, searching for any recognition. She was tall and thin, with dark hair. Leanne had no clue. Something in her peripheral vision grabbed her attention. A doctor's case.

"Is everything all right?" Surely nothing had happened while she was out at the barn.

Her mother smiled weakly. "Everything's fine, honey. Dr. Allen, this is my daughter, Leanne."

The doctor smiled, her hands busy putting away what looked like blood samples and medical paraphernalia. "It's a pleasure, Leanne. Your mother has been telling me all about the dude ranch you're going to open. That sounds very exciting."

She glanced at her mother, even more confused. "Did something happen while I was out?"

"Nothing happened. Dr. Allen needed blood samples for some tests."

"It wasn't easy convincing her, I can tell you," she said to Leanne, smiling. "I'm an internist. I'll be consulting with Dr. Baker."

Leanne stared at her in bewilderment. "Dr. Baker sent you here?" she asked, certain that couldn't be right. Dr. Baker would have told Leanne if an opportunity such as this had arisen.

Dr. Allen closed her case and straightened. "No, he didn't, but I will be sending him a full report on the results of these tests." She looked at Leanne's mother then. "I'll drop everything off at the lab in Bozeman. As soon as the results are in, Dr. Baker and

I will determine the best way to proceed with your case.''

"Thank you, Doctor," Joanna replied.

"Wait." Leanne moved between the woman and the door as she was about to leave without further explanation. "I want to know who sent you here." This went beyond bizarre.

"I'm sorry but I'm not at liberty to say who sent me." She smiled again, not even a hint of impatience showing. "Suffice it to say that it was the neighborly thing to do."

Ty.

Leanne couldn't even remember if she said good-bye to the doctor or to her mother. Before she could think what she was doing she'd driven halfway to the Cooper house. Who did he think he was sneaking around behind her back? She was furious. After only a couple of kisses he was already running her life. Making decisions for her. Butting in where he wasn't needed.

She slowed as she turned down the long drive, her thoughts darting from Ty to her mother. They might know soon exactly what was taking such a toll on her health. Suddenly all the fight drained out of Leanne. Dr. Allen was a specialist. Ty had obviously talked her into making a house call at no telling what kind of expense. Leanne parked her truck and for a full thirty seconds rested her forehead against the steering wheel.

He wanted to help.

He really cared, deeply.

She squeezed her eyes shut and tried her level best not to cry. She loved him so much for all that he'd done. Another emotion swelled in her chest. If she admitted the truth, she loved him for a whole lot more than that. She straightened, staring out the windshield at nothing at all. How could she keep pretending he wasn't the one for her?

He made her heart do those strange little somersaults.

He made her laugh.

He made her want him so badly that she'd been willing to have a one-night stand without any regrets.

He'd done everything he could to help her.

God, she did love him.

Really loved him.

Leanne shivered.

She supposed it could still be all about sex, but she was a great deal less certain of that now.

But what if he didn't love her that way? What if he only felt sorry for her?

She lifted her chin and pushed open the door. It didn't matter. If that doctor could help her mother, Leanne didn't care what motivated Ty to send her. Love, sympathy or whatever.

She was just so thankful.

Leanne raced to the house. She opened the front door and called out, "Anybody home?"

"In here," Mrs. Cooper called from the kitchen.

Leanne rushed to the kitchen doorway and beamed a smile. "Is Ty home?"

"I believe he is," the older woman said without looking up from her breadmaking. "Upstairs, I think."

Leanne pecked her cheek and rushed in the direction of the stairs. Mrs. Cooper called out something else behind her but Leanne was already halfway up the stairs. She'd drop back by the kitchen before she left. Right now she had to find Ty.

"Ty!" she called as soon as she cleared the top tread. "Ty!"

The sound of his voice reverberated from somewhere a few doors down.

"I need to talk to you!" she called out.

"Leanne?"

She smiled, desire curling inside her at the sound of his voice. It had come from the next door on the right. Leanne opened the door and burst inside. "Ty, I wanted—" The words that followed died in her throat as her eyes widened in disbelief.

Ty was chest-deep in steaming bathwater. She had just burst into the bathroom. Her knees almost buckled beneath her. How could she have forgotten that this was the bathroom? She'd played in this house dozens of times as a child.

"I...I..." Speech, as well as rational thought, eluded her as her eyes took in the details. He was naked, of course, steaming water lapping against that perfect chest. Those sinfully dark brown eyes were staring directly at her, daring her to come closer. Oh, God. She felt lightheaded. There was an excellent chance she might just faint.

His dark hair damp and swept back from that handsome face, Ty just grinned at her. "Planning on joining me?"

His words jolting her into action, she spun around, giving him her back. "I'm...I'm sorry. I didn't realize..." Lord have mercy. She had the abrupt, overwhelming urge to grab the nearest magazine and fan herself. It was sweltering in here.

"It's all right. Was there something you needed?" he asked, that sexy, smooth-as-glass voice enveloping her in a new kind of warmth, one that spread like wildfire through her trembling limbs.

She swallowed, difficult as that proved. "I wanted to thank you for sending the specialist to see my mother," she managed to say, her voice breaking only slightly. Emotion gathered in her throat. "I don't know how you managed it, but it really meant a lot to me." She looked down, squeezing her eyes shut to block the flood that threatened to unleash.

"Well," Ty began, his tone light, teasing almost, "if you can't lead a horse to water, then you just have to take the water to the horse."

Leanne couldn't help herself, she laughed at his misuse of the adage. "Works for me."

The sound of water sloshing in the tub made her jump. She stiffened, uncertain what she should do now. Was he getting out? Did she need to—

Strong fingers curled around her arms. "Relax," he murmured close to her ear. She could feel his body radiating heat right behind hers. "I don't bite."

Her breath trapped in her lungs when he turned her around to face him. She knew he was watching her, but she just couldn't help herself. Her gaze roved over that amazing body. He'd wrapped a towel around his hips, its hold there precarious at best. Water glistened on his skin. Damp, silky hair covered those sculpted pecs. She shivered visibly as a fresh wave of desire swirled inside her. A dozen snippets of memory, the feel of his mouth on hers, his strong body pressed against hers, his hungry touch, flashed through her mind, flooded her senses with a need so strong she could barely restrain the urge to reach out and touch him.

He stared deeply into her eyes and said, "You don't have to thank me."

"Ty, I…" She couldn't think with him looking at her that way, with his voice so gentle yet so thick with what she recognized as desire.

He reached up, cupped her face in one hand and stroked her cheek with his thumb. "But if you insist on thanking me, I prefer my gratitude in a more tangible form."

Time seemed to lapse into slow motion as his mouth descended toward hers. Uncertain of her ability to stay vertical, she braced her hands against his chest. The feel of his hot, damp skin beneath her palms only made bad matters worse. But she no longer cared. She wanted this kiss, wanted his touch more than anything else in the world at the moment. She wanted to take up where they'd left off after the dance last Friday night.

The electrifying pull started the moment their lips were a hairbreadth apart and Leanne knew that this time was somehow different from the others…the barriers were falling.

His mouth settled onto hers as he tenderly cradled her face with both hands. The gesture was so endearing that she thought her heart might not survive this one kiss.

He was like fire pulsing into her, devouring her and she couldn't get close enough. She felt his arousal against her belly and moved closer still. Her arms slid up around his neck and she leaned into him. The moisture from his skin was absorbed into her T-shirt. Her nipples pebbled in reaction to the feel of him.

His tongue thrust into her mouth. She gasped. He didn't back down; he kissed her harder.

Their ragged breathing echoed in the silent room as his hand glided down her throat, his fingers caressing all that they encountered until he clutched her breast. She groaned, or maybe it was Ty…

He drew back abruptly.

Leanne's hopes plummeted. Was he going to push her away again? Had she misread what she'd seen in his eyes? What she'd felt in his body? This couldn't happen again. Weak with disappointment, she could only stare into his eyes, a plea in her own.

He was breathless when he spoke. ''We have to…'' He searched her eyes as if as uncertain of her as she was of him. ''Go home. Wait for me.'' He kissed her lips one more time. ''One way or the other, we're going to finish this tonight.''

Leanne nodded, not sure whether his words were a promise or a threat.

She left the Cooper house and drove all the way home before she allowed herself to analyze what he'd said.

Tonight.

They would finish it tonight.

Chapter Eleven

Dex waited, none too patiently, until the family was gathered around the television preparing to watch the Friday evening lineup. All but Grandmother Cooper. Though she'd made herself comfortable along with the rest of the clan, she was deeply engrossed in her latest crocheting project. Dex had no idea what the bundles of yellow yarn would turn out to be when she finished, but he had a feeling it had something to do with her new grandchild on its way.

He couldn't help but smile at the sight of all of them together, munching on popcorn and waiting for the opening credits to pass. One big happy family. To the Montgomerys, family time consisted of going over stock reports. But, *this* kind of family time was kind of growing on him. His lips drew downward into a frown. But they weren't his family...not really. They treated him like family but that was only because they thought he was Ty.

How would this all turn out in the end? Would the Coopers be glad to find out who he really was? Would they accept him into their tight group as if he'd never left? Dex surveyed the big entry hall and considered that he'd spent the first few months of his life here. And no one suspected that he was back. Well, no one except Grandmother Cooper, and she hadn't mentioned it or behaved oddly, which led Dex to believe that perhaps he had misread her that night on the porch. Maybe she didn't know that he wasn't Ty.

Thoughts of Leanne intruded on his musings. He had to work this out somehow. She was driving him out of his mind. He wanted her more than he'd ever wanted anything before. *Anything.* And that was saying something. No woman had ever gotten to him like this.

He had to call Ty.

Dex picked up the telephone, and stretched the cord as far as it would go. He made it into the kitchen and barely far enough into the pantry to close the door. He listened for any sound coming from the family. He could vaguely make out the muffled voices from the television. Good. That meant that they couldn't overhear him as long as he didn't speak too loudly.

He quickly dialed the numbers. Now, if he could only fool whoever answered the phone.

"Montgomery residence." A soft feminine voice announced on the other end of the line.

His grandmother. A surge of emotion rendered Dex speechless for several seconds. He hadn't realized until that precise moment how much he'd missed her. Almost two weeks he'd been gone. Did she suspect that Ty wasn't the man she'd raised as her son? If he told her right now that he was Dex would she be glad to hear his voice? How were they getting along without him?

He let go a breath. Ty was there. He'd been there

the whole time. They were obviously as fooled as the Coopers. They didn't miss Dex. They didn't even realize he was gone.

"Hello," she repeated. "Is anyone there?"

He quickly summoned a voice that in no way resembled his own. "Dex Montgomery, please," he told her, satisfied at how un-Dex he sounded.

To his utter relief she didn't ask who was calling. Instead, she asked him to hold and laid the telephone down. He heard the sound of her high-heeled shoes clicking on the marble floor of the foyer as she went in search of Ty. Another wave of emotion overtook him. He closed his eyes and envisioned the home in which he'd lived for as long as he could remember. And suddenly he wished he was there. He wanted to sit in his grandfather's study and discuss business while his grandfather nursed his favorite pipe, though he'd given up smoking it some time ago. Dex loved that pipe.

Or Dex could go out to the greenhouse and watch his Grandmother Montgomery with her roses and African violets. She had quite the green thumb. Grandmother Cooper tending her flowerbeds reminded him of home. At least the two women had one thing in common. Of course he couldn't see Grandmother Cooper going off to a friendly game of dice on Sunday nights. It was his Grandmother Montgomery's one vice.

"Hello."

The voice that echoed over the line this time was a carbon copy of Dex's, except for the slightest hint of a Western drawl. Dex grinned. He wondered how his brother had explained that slight change in inflection. Or maybe he'd carefully controlled his speech pattern and had only unknowingly dropped his guard for a moment.

"Ty, it's Dex."

"Thank God it's you." Ty sounded immensely relieved. "I was afraid it would be someone I should recognize and I wouldn't. Doggone if this trading places business isn't some flat-out nerve-rattling work."

"I know exactly how you feel."

"Is everything all right?" his brother wanted to know, a twinge of worry in his voice.

Dex gave him a quick rundown of how everyone was doing, including the news about Chad and Jenny's pregnancy. Ty followed suit, explaining that the Montgomerys were doing well and didn't appear to suspect a thing. George, however, was another story. Ty was pretty sure George knew he wasn't Dex.

"Don't admit anything," Dex warned him. "George always played those mind games to get the truth out of me when I was a teenager. If you give him an inch he'll take a mile. He's relentless like that." He sorely missed George. Missed them all, truth be told.

A stretch of silence lingered between them for a time.

"I think I've met someone," Ty finally said, quietly, solemnly.

Dex frowned. Surely Bridget hadn't gotten to him. Ty definitely was not in her league. She would eat him alive. "I thought you were going to keep Bridget busy with—"

"It's not Bridget. It's Jessica Stovall." It would

have been impossible to miss the excitement in Ty's voice when he talked about her.

Uh-oh. "What about Leanne?" Dex felt compelled to demand. She was falling for Ty…well, for *him,* but she thought he was Ty. And here Ty was off falling for someone down in Atlanta. Anger twisted inside Dex. He didn't want Leanne hurt in all this. If Ty had ever made her believe for one moment…

"I told you," Ty interrupted Dex's runaway thoughts. "We're just friends. Leanne is like a sister to me. Nothing else."

His words stemmed the fury a bit. "So, there has never been anything between the two of you?" Dex persisted. He would have a definite answer. If there ever had been, then Ty would have to make it right. Dex would see to it.

"Never," Ty assured him. "Friends, that's all. Anything else you may have heard is only wishful thinking on our folks' part. I swear."

Another reign of silence stood between them for two long beats.

"Wait one cotton-picking minute," Ty said suddenly. "Are you and Leanne…?" He swore. A string of words that didn't bear repeating followed. "Don't even think about breaking that girl's heart. Do you hear me, Dex? I won't have it."

Dex's fury renewed itself. "I didn't come here to break any hearts," he said tightly.

"Then what the hell's going on? Why all the questions about me and Leanne?" Ty snapped right back.

"It's nothing for you to be concerned about. I won't do anything I can't *undo.*" Dex prayed that was true. Hadn't he already done things he wouldn't be able to undo?

"I'm counting on that," Ty told him bluntly. "This isn't about revenge of any sort."

"You're right," Dex allowed. "It's about…" His brow lined in confusion. He didn't know what it was about. He'd lost all focus this past week. "It's about understanding the past," he finally said.

"Yeah," Ty agreed. "It's about the past."

"Call me if you need anything," Dex offered. "Or if you decide it's time to have our big announcement."

"I will." Ty cleared his throat. *"Soon."*

Dex sneaked out of the pantry and quietly replaced the phone on the hall table. He tried not to wonder what Ty had meant by *soon.* Was he weary of this ruse already? Or did he simply miss his family? Dex had no intention of setting a precise date until he'd learned all he wanted to know…satisfied his curiosity. And certainly not until he'd settled things with Leanne.

Dex retrieved his hat and keys. One thing was certain, he definitely missed his family, even if he hadn't actually realized it until he heard his Grandmother Montgomery's voice.

But for right now he couldn't think about any of that. He had to straighten this thing out with Leanne before they went too far. He had no intention of doing what she clearly wanted him to…what *he* wanted to.

He had to end this tonight.

After a quick good night to the Coopers, he headed to Leanne's. Before he arrived he had to come up with a plausible excuse—one that wouldn't hurt her feelings—for putting the brakes on this thing between them.

She would understand.

He was certain of it.

LEANNE HAD TRIED ON everything she owned, which didn't take long, yet the decision as to what to wear seemed monumental. Finally she had picked the only dress besides the blue one that halfway complemented her figure, and made her feel feminine.

The white dress was old, but she'd always loved the fact that it buttoned up the front. It was long and filmy, with a hem that hit mid-calf and fabric that showed off her curves. Her skin was tanned just enough from working outside on the ranch to contrast nicely with the white. She'd left her hair down, but braided it in a long, loose style. Her old leather sandals were the only pair she owned, but they too were feminine looking. She smiled at her pink toenails. She'd even taken the time to do her nails. She flared her fingers and admired the short but freshly manicured tips. She didn't own any fancy jewelry or perfume, but she'd applied a smidgen of the strawberry-scented spray she saved for special occasions.

Now, Leanne stood back and studied her appearance. Her cheeks were flushed with anticipation, her eyes glistened with the desire she couldn't seem to hide. Even her mother had noticed the change. Was this what love was supposed to be like?

This overwhelming need to be with someone, that twist in her stomach each time she thought of him. She felt like such a child compared to Ty. He was thirty-two, and, considering his charming personality and handsome looks, she was certain he'd had his share of women. What on earth would a naive virgin have to offer him? She frowned. Yet he seemed interested enough. When he kissed her, touched her, it felt like he wanted her. Could she be reading too much into his reaction?

She let go a big breath. She was nearly certain that this was a mistake. She wasn't supposed to fall in love with Ty. She couldn't possibly be the kind of wife he wanted…she had other plans. Plans he now knew about.

Maybe he didn't want her for a wife.

Leanne chewed her lower lip and tried to rationalize that thought. He'd given absolutely no indication that he felt their folks were right and that they belonged together. In fact, he hadn't talked about the future at all.

Maybe he only wanted what she'd thought she wanted. Just to be with him. But she knew Ty better than that. He would never take advantage of her. Considering the vibes she'd been giving off lately, he most likely thought she was the one who wanted a future together or, at the very least, wanted to have sex with him.

What a predicament. She didn't know what she wanted. Should they just go with what their hearts told them and not question it? Would it be a mistake? It would. She was pretty sure of it. Ty would be extremely upset when he realized she hadn't been with anyone else. He would feel obligated to do the right thing…or stop.

Leanne moistened her lips. Then there was only one thing to do. She had to make him believe that she wasn't a virgin…at least until it was too late to change his mind. She would have this one night whatever the future held for the two of them. If this whole thing was simply about sex, then she would soon know it. She was through waiting for life to happen. Starting from this moment she was going to make it happen.

Her way.

Decision reached, Leanne made her way to the living room to check on her mother. Joanna was knitting a cap and sweater set for the coming addition to the Cooper family. Another twinge of anxiety plagued Leanne. What was it about babies lately that made her feel so anxious?

At least her mother was feeling well enough to expend a little energy. For that Leanne was extremely grateful. By next week Dr. Allen might even have some news or suggested treatment that could turn her mother's life around. That would make things perfect.

Just perfect.

"Can I get you anything, Mama?"

Joanna looked up. "I'm fine, child." Her eyebrows lifted a fraction. "My, don't you look lovely. Do you have another date with Ty?"

Leanne shook her head. "Not a date."

Joanna turned back to her knitting. "Um-hm."

Leanne started to insist that her mother was making something of nothing but a knock at the door stopped her. She gasped. Her mother eyed her even more suspiciously. Leanne marched to the door, cursing herself for being so transparent.

Ty stood in the open doorway looking more handsome than ever. Maybe it was the faded chambray shirt or the worn jeans that gloved his body so well. Whatever it was, he took her breath away.

The damp hair that had glistened when she'd walked in on his bath was now dry and combed neatly into place. But time and distance since their encounter had done nothing to lessen the intensity in those brown eyes. He looked every bit as hungry as she felt.

Then he smiled and her heart did one of those crazy flip-flops that sent warning bells off inside her head.

"Well, don't just stand there, Leanne," her mother scolded. "Ask him to come in."

If her mother only knew, Leanne thought. She planned to invite Ty a lot farther than simply inside her home.

"Come in," she murmured, stepping back to open the door wider.

Hat in hand, he came inside, and Leanne was struck all over again by how good he looked. Handsome as sin, with mile-wide shoulders. Why had she never noticed those wonderfully muscular thighs before or that equally well-formed behind?

He flashed a smile at her then turned to her mother. "How are you feeling this evening, Mrs. Watley?"

"Real fine, Ty." She literally beamed at him. "I'm mighty grateful for that fancy doc you sent out here to see me, but I'm awful worried that you shouldn't have done such a generous thing."

"Dr. Allen owed me a favor," he assured her. "She was happy to relieve herself of that debt."

Leanne frowned. How was it that Dr. Allen owed Ty a favor? He'd apparently made a lot more friends during his trip to the city than she could ever have imagined. She felt a stab of jealousy. What if the pretty doctor and Ty had...? She had no way of knowing for sure how Ty knew the doctor. It was pointless to get all worked up for no real reason. Ty was both charming and persuasive. He made friends easily. She couldn't know all his friends, she assured herself. And she would not let foolish thoughts ruin this evening.

He turned to Leanne then. "I thought we could take a drive." He shrugged, the gesture seeming as hopeful as nonchalant. "To talk."

A shiver trembled through her. "Sure."

Dex watched as Leanne kissed her mother and picked up her purse and then rejoined him at the door. "I'm driving," she said, then smiled, the expression tremulous. He suddenly wanted to hold her and tell her that everything would be all right. That *he* would make it so. But he wasn't at all sure he could do that.

Once in her truck, Leanne drove in virtual silence until they reached the destination she had in mind. For the first time since his arrival Dex longed for his Mercedes. He'd like to take her someplace special in real style.

The sun was beginning to melt along the top of the mountain ranges in the distance. For one long moment, he couldn't take his eyes off the view. They'd driven up a long, meandering slope until they reached a grassy plateau which overlooked the river that flowed across Cooper property. Dex felt reasonably sure its beauty rivaled any other place on earth he'd visited.

"This place is amazing," he murmured.

She nodded. "It's my favorite place in the whole

world." She looked at him then. "I come here when I want to be alone to think."

At that moment he would have given any price to know what she thought about when she was all alone. "I can see why. It's..." He peered out over the natural beauty before him. "...perfect." And they didn't need a Mercedes to make it that way.

"Haven't you ever stopped on this ridge just to enjoy the view?"

He shook his head, hoping she'd take it as a no, he'd never taken the time, instead of the no he meant, which was he'd never been here before in his life.

"Come on."

As she opened her door she grabbed the blanket he'd noticed on the seat when he got into her truck. She'd insisted on driving. Since she knew where she wanted to go, that had been fine with him. Now he wondered if that had been a mistake. Leanne appeared to be a little too prepared.

No matter what else happened, he had to do this right.

He watched as she spread the blanket on the ground. The white dress she wore showed off her golden skin. The long, thick braid she'd twisted her hair into fell over her shoulder making him yearn to release it so that he could run his hands through all that silky hair. The dress buttoned up the front, but the top two buttons were unfastened leaving the barest peek at cleavage. His mouth went dust-dry.

After the blanket was smoothed to her satisfaction, she sat down and tossed her purse to the side. Hesitant but unsure what else he could do at this point, Dex joined her.

"This is nice," he commented, his attention focused once more on the sun as it slipped slowly behind the mountains.

"It sure is." She pulled her knees up to her chest, the long dress cascading down to cover everything but her sandal-clad feet. She sighed contentedly.

Dex's gaze zeroed in on those sexy pink toenails and he suddenly wanted to kiss her there. He blinked, dispelling the arousing image of him kissing his way up her long, slender legs.

For several minutes they sat in complete silence. Dex tried desperately to keep his mind on the fact that he would be leaving soon and that he couldn't possibly do anything that couldn't be undone. *This* definitely couldn't be undone. He was certain of that, if nothing else. He would not hurt Leanne. He simply wouldn't do it.

Daylight faded little by little, taking the sun's warmth with it. Leanne chafed her arms with her hands.

"Are you cold?" Dammit, why hadn't he thought to bring a jacket or something?

She smiled, his pulse reacted. "No. I'm okay."

Oh no! He saw in her eyes the one thing he definitely hadn't wanted to see right now: desire.

"Leanne," he began, knowing he couldn't delay this any longer. He had to do something or risk making a terrible mistake. "There's something you have to know."

How was he supposed to tell her that he wanted her desperately but that it couldn't possibly work? He wasn't who she thought he was. He was an impostor. He flinched at the realization.

She held up a hand to stop him before he continued. "Wait." She quickly fished in her purse for something, palmed it before he could see what it was, then turned back to him. Too close...entirely too close, but he couldn't bring himself to move away. It was too much to ask.

"Leanne—"

"Don't say anything," she pressed her fingers to his lips. "I don't want this to be about talking."

She kissed him. He tensed, tried not to respond, but he was only human. A few seconds of that sweet mouth on his and he had to kiss her back. She rested her small hands against his chest, her touch made need surge hard and fast inside him. Slowly, her cool fingers trembling slightly, she released first one, then another of his shirt's buttons. Her efficient fingers moved lower, until she'd opened it to his waist. She reached inside and touched his bare skin. He groaned in spite of his promise to himself that he wouldn't let this happen.

He held back as long as he could, but she was pushing him harder and harder with that hot little mouth and those exploring fingers. His hands went to her face. He sagged with the relief of simply touching her soft skin. She ushered him down onto the blanket. He didn't resist. Couldn't have if he'd wanted to. Her tongue ventured into his mouth, then retreated. He did the same to her, daring her to come back for more. She grew bolder, straddling his waist, the long dress pushed up around her thighs now. She dragged his hands down to her breasts. He cupped them instinctively. She moaned and ground that fiery heat between her thighs into him. Any control he had left crumbled.

She quickly released several of her own buttons. His hands slid immediately inside her dress. He toyed with her nipples, awed at the tight little buds beneath his fingers. She broke the kiss, arched her back, pressing her breasts more firmly into his palms.

Dex watched her. Couldn't catch his breath at what he saw. She was beautiful sitting astride him, her head thrown back in ecstasy, her full breasts bared to him. She'd come here with the intention of offering herself to him. She wanted this. A new wave of desire roared through him. He wanted this.

But it was wrong.

She thought...

He rolled her over, putting himself in the dominant position in an attempt to regain control. His loins throbbed as his arousal pressed into her softness. He swallowed hard and forced himself to think. He had to think.

"Leanne, this would be a mistake for both of us," he said as calmly as he could, considering his voice was rough with need.

She shook her head. "No. We're adults. This doesn't have to be about the future or the family. It only has to be about here and now. About the need we have."

"You don't understand," he pleaded. She wasn't making this easy. "There are things you don't know. I can't—"

She shushed him with her fingers again. "I don't care. I want this. I know you do, too." She arched her hips against his. "I can feel how much you want this."

He closed his eyes for three long beats in an effort to slow his body's plunge toward the point of no return. It didn't work. When he looked at her again, he still wanted her with an intensity that shook him to the core of his being.

How could he say no?

He opened his mouth to try, but she stopped him with another of those hungry kisses. This time it went on and on until they were both gasping for breath.

A new reality peeked through the haze. He groaned. "But I don't have any protection," he whispered between her fevered kisses, disappointed rather than relieved as he should be.

Her mouth still taunting his, she groped around the blanket until she found what she searched for. She thrust the tiny packet into his hand.

"Here," she murmured, breathless. "I came prepared."

He looked at her for a time, unable to speak or move. She wanted him badly enough to make it happen. How could he disappoint her? How could he...

"Please don't make me wait any longer." The plea was punctuated by flames so hot in her eyes that they seared straight through him.

"You won't have to wait." He kissed her hard, with all the raging emotions bottled up inside him. He wanted her. He would have her. Now.

He kissed his way down her torso, opening more buttons as he went. She writhed and made tiny gasping sounds in his wake. He loved it. She only made him want to please her more. This would be about her, he decided then and there. All about her.

When her dress was open all the way down and her voluptuous body exposed fully to him, he sat back on his haunches and removed his shirt, all the while admiring every beautiful detail of her. She watched him, her eyes wide with anticipation and maybe a tiny bit of apprehension. When their gazes locked, she closed her eyes and took a deep breath, her perfect breasts rising and falling with the effort.

He unfastened his jeans, the sound of the zipper making her shiver and urging him on. He pushed his jeans and boxers down, the rasp of denim against flesh provoking another of those little shivers in her. He ripped the foil packet, and watched for the next reaction; she sucked in a sharp breath. Need pulsed through him, forcing him toward the edge of control. He slipped on the condom she'd given him and lowered his body over hers. She gasped, her warm breath eventually feathering across his jaw when she relaxed.

With painstaking slowness he kissed her lips, then made a path down her throat. Her fingers threaded into his hair and ushered him to her breasts. He took his time there, pleasuring her until she once more writhed beneath him, her breath so ragged he felt certain she might climax even before he entered her. Slowly he continued down to her hips. He dragged her panties along her legs, leaving a path of hot kisses, garnering more of those sweet little shivers. When he loomed over her once more, his arousal nestled against her mound. She arched upward, crying out with need.

When he would have reached for that place that

ached so for him, she pushed his hand away and grasped the part of him that throbbed for her. She guided him to her entrance, too needy to bother with more foreplay.

"Now?" he murmured the question against her lips, then kissed them.

She nodded. "Hurry!"

He pushed inside only a fraction. He wanted this tension to last…to mount until they both screamed with satisfaction.

Her expression taut with anticipation, she wriggled her hips, then locked her legs around his and arched upward forcing him inside one more hot, tight inch. She was so tight. It was all he could do not to thrust fully. The blood roared in his ears. His heart pounded so hard he could scarcely breathe, but he held back…making it last. His mouth found and melded with hers, his tongue thrust inside. He mimicked the move with his hips, withdrawing slightly then pushing deeper, just another inch, but he met with more resistance. Confusion buzzed into his thoughts. Desire pounded through his veins, making coherent thought impossible. He was on the brink of release and he wasn't even fully inside her yet. He was going crazy hovering somewhere between hesitation and desperation. But something was wrong.

He pulled back once more, pushed inside again. Realization crashed into his skull this time. He drew back from the kiss and stared into her startled gaze. He shook his head, unable to believe what his body was telling him.

"Don't stop," she urged, trying with all her might to pull him back down to her.

"You...this..." He shook his head again. "You're..."

He saw the determination in her eyes a split second before she acted on it. She surged upward with her hips, taking him past the barrier. They cried out together, the barrage of sensations overwhelming. Instinctively he plunged deeply inside her, then held perfectly still.

"I...shouldn't have..." he stammered, hardly believing what he'd allowed to happen. His whole body strummed with need. He wanted to drive toward release, but he had to hold back. Had to give her time...

She was breathing hard and fast, her eyes far too bright for his liking, even in the dwindling daylight.

"Are you all right?" he murmured.

She moved her head from side to side, her lips trembling.

Dex tensed. He swallowed with enormous difficulty. He was throbbing inside her. Her tight feminine muscles were pulsing around him, making him want to start that ancient rhythm without further delay. "I..." he began, uncertain of what to say or do. He'd damned sure never had this problem before. He wanted her so badly, but he had to be sure this was what she wanted.

She shifted her hips beneath him. "I'll be all right if you'll do what you're supposed to." She squirmed some more. "Please."

She looked so vulnerable, yet she wanted to be so brave. She'd allowed him to think she'd done this before...allowed him to fall into her tender trap. And he'd wanted to. Wanted to more than he'd wanted his next breath.

His lips found hers and then nothing else mattered. Slowly he found the pace that was exactly what they both needed. He would do what he'd intended only moments ago. He'd make this night about her.

Soon, too soon, they cried out together.

And no matter how wrong it was, it felt absolutely right.

Chapter Twelve

Leanne hefted the bags of groceries onto the passenger side of her truck seat. She let go a sigh of relief and closed the door. Thoughts of Ty suddenly making her step light, she quickly skirted the hood to reach the driver's-side door.

The last few days had been perfect. Her hand stilled on the door handle as a wave of warmth washed over her. She and Ty had made love several more times since the first time. He'd been so sweet and gentle with her, and yet, his tenderness had in no way lessened his amazing skill. Though she had no guide by which to judge, she was certain that Ty was a truly masterful lover. Her stomach quivered with memories from their first time. He'd regretted taking her virginity, at least at first. Then he'd turned extremely possessive. She smiled. She liked that part.

Caution had been his watchword ever since. She always had to initiate their lovemaking. He never pushed her in any way. He was so hesitant at times that she feared this whole thing between them was one-sided. But then he would prove her wrong with his wildly intense lovemaking. It was during those intimate sessions when his soul was bared to her and he was at his most vulnerable that she could see how deep his feelings were.

It scared her to death, only because she was so uncertain of her own ground. She'd been so sure for so long that she and Ty weren't right for each, this complete turnaround frightened her beyond reason.

It had to be right.

It felt right...most of the time, anyway.

Forcing her attention back to the present, Leanne reminded herself that she had to get home, because the doctor was supposed to call with news about her mother. Not to mention she had to put the groceries away and go over to the Coopers to visit Jenny. She felt guilty for not having dropped by already. They were neighbors and friends, after all. Leanne needed to congratulate her personally.

She pressed a hand to her stomach and wondered what it would be like to be carrying Ty's child. Butterflies took flight beneath her belly button, sending wispy sensations all through her. She shook herself. She was definitely moving too fast for comfort.

"Leanne!"

She turned at the sound of her name. Mrs. Paula waved from the door of her shop. Leanne threw up her hand and produced a smile. Lordy, what did she want? She'd never get home if she let herself be dragged into a conversation with the inquisitive, however well-meaning, woman.

"Come into the shop for a minute or two," Mrs. Paula insisted. "I have something to show you."

"Yes, ma'am," Leanne said, reluctance slowing

her. Though she kept her smile in place, her pleasant mood wilted. She'd never get away.

"I got a new bridal catalog," the woman enthused as Leanne followed her into the shop. "You've just got to see the lovely dresses for this season."

Bridal catalog? Leanne's eyes went wide. Had word that she and Ty had…? Her stomach knotted with worry. Surely not. They'd been so discreet—for the most part anyway.

Mrs. Paula ushered her to the counter. "You know a June wedding is always the best. We've still got time to plan one if we start now." She patted Leanne on the arm. "Did you know that I'm a wedding planner, too?"

Leanne's stomach plunged for parts south. Oh, God. If Mrs. Paula thought she and Ty were a couple, the whole town must as well or would very soon.

"Mrs. Paula, I'm certain there's been some sort of mistake," she said, her voice strained with anxiety and a touch of embarrassment. "I haven't even been proposed to."

Mrs. Paula gave her another of those affectionate pats. "Not to worry, dear. The proposal's just a formality. We all know where the two of you are headed." She took Leanne's chin between her thumb and forefinger. "Why just look at that face," she cooed. "Anyone with eyes can see you're a woman in love. And the whole town knows how Ty has been wooing you."

She released Leanne and glanced covertly from side to side. "I hear tell that he spends most of his time at your place." She winked. "Helping you out. And everybody saw the two of you on the dance floor last Friday night. Why, you couldn't have got a pin between y'uns without drawing blood. Gracious, I've never seen such a kiss.''

Leanne had to get out of there. Anything she said at this point was only going to make bad matters worse.

"Now you come on over here, little miss, I have just the perfect dress in mind for you.''

The bell on the shop entrance jingled. Leanne turned at the same time as a shrill feminine voice called, ''Yoo-hoo!''

Agnes Washburn and Corine Miller scurried toward Leanne and Mrs. Paula, both outfitted in their Sunday clothes, hat and gloves included. Leanne suffered a moment of outright panic. If these two got wind—

"Paula called and told us you were right outside her shop. We came as fast as we could,'' Ms. Washburn exclaimed.

"Have you shown her the one we like yet, Paula?'' Ms. Miller inquired. ''It's on page hundred and fourteen.''

"I was just getting to that,'' Paula assured her friend.

Too late…they knew.

Leanne had to warn Ty.

DEX WAS DESPERATE to keep himself occupied, thus the rearranging of hay bales. He had already groomed Dodger and any other horse in the barn that would stand still for him. His efforts had been to no avail. He couldn't seem to work off the restless energy pumping through him.

He paused, grabbed the shirt he'd discarded and wiped his damp brow with it. There was no getting around it. He'd painted himself into a corner on this one—literally. Dex dropped onto a nearby bale and let go a weary breath. He'd only wanted to help make her dream of starting the dude ranch come true. He hadn't meant to complicate the issue. But complicated it was.

He couldn't sleep…he couldn't eat. All he thought about was Leanne. He didn't dare label the feelings she engendered in him, but he knew something special when he experienced it. Surrendering, he closed his eyes and allowed the memories that he'd worked so hard all morning to keep at bay to overtake him.

Making love to her had sealed his fate. He'd made love with lots of different women, but no one had made him feel this way.

Not even close.

With every fiber of his being he wanted to possess her completely…wanted to make her his. All that made him male roared with the need to claim her as his alone. It shook him as nothing else ever had.

He looked around the huge hayloft and tried to reconcile any part of this with who he was. It was impossible. Absolutely impossible.

He closed his eyes and unsuccessfully attempted to block the thought that always haunted him: what would she do when she discovered the truth?

He wasn't the man she thought he was. Dex, he reminded himself, not Ty. The very idea of seeing the pain in her eyes that reality would bring tore him apart inside. But how could he stop her from finding out? He couldn't. She would soon know the truth.

Soon. His conversation with Ty a few days ago echoed in his ears. It would all be over soon.

Dex swore softly. There was an ache building inside him that threatened to shatter all that he'd ever been or hoped to be. He didn't know what he wanted anymore...who he was. Not really. Helping Leanne's mother had made him realize how badly he missed practicing medicine as an intern. But his medical degree had never been about practicing medicine. Yet a part of him yearned to do just that, at least on some level.

His grandfather Montgomery would have a stroke if Dex even mentioned such a thing.

And what about the family here? How would the Coopers take his big announcement when the time came? Why hadn't he and Ty thought of all this before they set this charade into motion? He was a fool, that's what he was. He was supposed to have come here to find the truth about his parents and maybe show these people what a mistake they had made. He swore again. Where was the full measure of bitterness he'd anticipated feeling? Where were the ugly, hidden secrets he'd expected to uncover? Instead he'd found pictures of his father at a time when he had obviously been the happiest of his entire life.

Here...with these people.

And he'd found the letters.

It was time he looked at them. He wiped his hands on his denim-clad thighs and reached into his back pocket. He'd been carrying the small bundle around with him for days trying to work up the nerve to read them.

It was time.

He untied the delicate pink ribbon and opened the first envelope.

My dearest Tara…

By the time Dex finished the fourth and final letter his heart was aching as it never had before. His father had loved his mother more than Dex could ever have imagined. There had been some kind of rift between the families years ago. Something about money. Chuck had wanted to be with Tara anyway. Apparently they'd eventually found a way.

This had been their home.

Dex swiped the emotion from his eyes with the back of his hand. He retied the ribbon and tucked the letters back into his pocket until he could put the precious memories away where they belonged. His father had loved these people. And he was falling in love with them, too.

Love?

He laughed at the irony of it. Love. He was a businessman. He made business decisions on cold hard facts. He never relied on gut instinct alone. Emotion never entered into the equation. None of this was real.

He was simply playing a part. Getting into character. He was supposed to be Ty. He'd worked hard to fit in, master his role. All these confusing feelings would be expected from a man like Ty, he reasoned. Dex was only behaving as he believed his brother would. None of this was real.

That statement left a bad taste in his mouth. But it was true, wasn't it?

Soon he would be back in Atlanta and back to his old self.

He clenched his jaw hard.

But not today.

The memory of touching Leanne, tasting her…being inside her took his breath away, made him want to forget who he was for a little while longer.

Today he was Ty Cooper.

"Ty!"

Dex jerked from his troubling thoughts. Chad and Court had joined him in the loft. He stood and faced them. "What's up?" He knew a moment of disconcertion as their solemn gazes settled on him. Had he made a wrong step—one he didn't know about?

Chad shrugged, his expression suddenly sheepish. "Look, I wanted to apologize for ragging you so much about acting a little strange since you got back from your trip."

"We know you've had a lot on your mind," Court chimed in. "We just wanted you to know how proud of you we are."

Dex looked from one to the other and tried his level best to read between the lines. "Well…ah…thanks, guys."

"It was really something how you found that doctor for Mrs. Watley and all," Court continued. "Gran says she's going to fully recover."

"What?" This was news to Dex. Why hadn't Leanne told him?

Chad nodded. "Just before Gran left for town Mrs. Watley gave her the good news. I don't think Leanne even knows yet. Mrs. Watley thought she might be over here."

Relief and a kind of satisfaction, so profound, flooded Dex to the point that he thought he might have to sit down. "That's great," he managed to say.

Court hugged him suddenly. "You did good, brother. We're proud of you."

Chad took his turn with the bear-hug act. "Oh, yeah." He drew away and reached into his back pocket. "Something came in the mail for you." He handed Dex a business-size envelope. "I thought it might be from those investors."

Dex stared at the return address on the envelope, Dyson Brothers. He recognized the five-star restaurant chain. Ty had clearly been aiming high with his future plans. His lips formed a grim line as he ripped the envelope open. He knew what it contained before he opened it though. It would be a rejection. Accepted proposals didn't come in the form of a one-page letter.

He read the short, to-the-point letter, then blew out a heavy breath. Ty would be immensely disappointed. "They passed on the deal," he told his brothers.

While they were giving him sympathetic pats on the back and assuring him that something else would work out, Dex was stunned by his own mental slip. He'd just thought of Chad and Court as his brothers as if it was the most natural thing in the world.

And somehow, deep inside him, he knew it was.

His father would have wanted it that way.

LEANNE PARKED in front of the Cooper house and just sat there for a few moments. Her mind still reeled with all that had taken place in Mrs. Paula's shop.

She had to tell Ty. The whole thing had gotten out of hand.

She also needed to warn him that she was probably falling in love with him and she had no idea how to stop it. She groaned. She couldn't tell him that…especially considering she couldn't be sure that he felt the same way. Leanne climbed out of the truck, disgusted with herself and the whole blooming town.

This wasn't supposed to happen.

She was so confused…so very confused.

Worry slowing her, she trudged up the steps and across the porch. Maybe things would work out somehow. Lord knew she wanted Ty. The thought of spending every night in his arms…of having his children, made her feel all warm and tingly inside. But there was so much to iron out before she could go there. Not the least of which was figuring out if he felt even remotely the same way.

She opened the front door and poked her head inside. "Anybody home?"

A glowing Jenny hurried from the family room to greet her. They hugged, tears filling Leanne's eyes. She was so happy for Jenny.

When at last they drew apart, Leanne said, "You look wonderful. I'm so proud for you and Chad."

"Visit with me awhile. Brenda and the kids are in the backyard." Jenny hooked her arm in Leanne's and led her to the dining room to sit down at the table. "We can't wait. Angelica's a little upset about it, but she'll come around."

"Sure she will," Leanne agreed. "She'll be a terrific big sister."

Jenny clutched Leanne's hand. "So tell me if

there's any truth to all the rumors I'm hearing about you and Ty.'' She winked. "Ty won't say a word."

Leanne resisted the urge to sigh out loud. She'd just bet Ty wouldn't. He most likely felt as trapped as she did...well maybe *trapped* wasn't the right word.

"I want to help plan the wedding," Jenny announced, bubbling with excitement. "We all do. Gran and Brenda are so excited, too. Gran's in town for a little shopping, otherwise she'd be in here."

How would Leanne ever get this runaway train back on track? "I think it's a little early to start planning a wedding," she suggested. "There hasn't been a proposal yet. To be honest I'm not sure there will be one."

Jenny dismissed that technicality with a wave of her hand. "You know how pig-headed Ty can be. He'll keep us all in suspense until he's good and ready to do it."

Leanne chewed her lower lip. "I think everyone has the wrong impression, Ty and I have been working together—"

"Oh, honey, *pleeeze.*" Jenny leaned across the table. "I don't think there's any way anyone could have gotten the wrong impression if they saw you two together at the dance."

Leanne forced her right leg to stop its sudden bouncing. "Well, that's not..." How did she explain?

Jenny shook her head. "I can tell you're in love. I can see it in your eyes." She grinned. "I can also tell that you've already been *together,* if you know what I mean."

Leanne blushed to the roots of her hair and maybe beyond. "I...we..." What could she say? It was true.

Jenny patted her hand. "Don't even try to deny it. Even if I couldn't see it written all over your face. I can see it on Ty's. Every time he looks at you or your name is mentioned, you can see the territorial gleam in his eyes."

Leanne managed a trembling smile. "That's good to know." At least Ty was as transparent as she was.

"Who knows?" Jenny offered cheerily. "There could be a little one on the way already."

Another rush of heat claimed Leanne's face. They'd only failed to use protection once. "Jenny—"

Again Jenny dismissed anything she would have said with a flippant wave of her hand. "Don't sweat it. Angelica was on the way when Chad and I got married. We haven't regretted it for a moment."

"We haven't talked about children yet," Leanne stammered. She'd never known that about Jenny and Chad. She frowned, mentally doing the math and finding herself shocked all over again.

"Well, you know the Cooper men. They love to breed." Jenny's eyes twinkled. "I'm definitely not complaining, mind you. Ty will want to start right away I'm sure."

Leanne squirmed in her seat, weighing the consequences of simply jumping up and running out of the house. "I have the dude ranch to get off the ground," she countered, suddenly feeling the precise definition of *trapped*.

"Oh, Ty will find someone to run that for you. Being Mrs. Ty Cooper will take up far too much of your time for you to worry about running anything. Once those babies start coming you won't have time to think of anything else.''

A cold, hard knot formed in Leanne's stomach. Hyperventilation seemed a definite possibility. ''Speaking of Ty.'' Leanne stood abruptly. ''Do you know where he is? I need to talk to him.''

''I think he's out in the barn.'' Jenny followed her to the back door, reluctant to let her go. ''When you're through talking to your honey, come on back in here and let's map out that wedding.''

Leanne only nodded.

Before the door closed behind her, she broke into a run. She ran all the way to the barn, skidding to a halt when she almost ran headlong into Court and Chad as they strolled through the double doors.

''Don't worry, Leanne,'' Chad teased with a wink. ''He's still in there. We didn't let him get away.''

The two laughed as they headed toward the house. Leanne felt suddenly sick to her stomach. Her hands shook as she tucked a loose strand of hair behind her ear. Her groceries would just have to wait. She had to straighten all this out first. Then she had to get home. She didn't want to miss the doctor's call.

Leanne found Ty just inside the barn door reading what appeared to be a crumpled letter. He stood as still as stone only a few feet away, his angled jaw rigid, his dark hair tousled. Her heart started to pound immediately. His hat was missing, which struck her once again as so unlike Ty. His shirt was completely unbuttoned and hanging open. As usual the fit of his jeans made her feel giddy. She fought for her next breath. Her chest ached with longing, but she pushed it away. She had to do this. She couldn't let things between them keep spiraling out of control. It had already gone way too far. And it was her fault. He'd tried to slow things down...to steer away from physical intimacy. But she'd forced the issue. She had to make it right now.

"Ty," she said, then paused to dredge up enough strength to keep the quiver out of her voice.

He turned toward her, a smile instantly lighting his handsome face. "Leanne, I was just thinking about you. Have you—"

"We need to talk," she cut him off. She moistened her lips and forced her feet to cover the distance between them.

Shoving the letter into his jeans pocket, he met her halfway. "Sure." As if it were as natural a reflex as breathing, he leaned down and kissed her. He didn't linger, just a quick, tender kiss that stirred that ache building inside her. It affected her so deeply she wasn't sure she would be able to do what she knew she had to.

"Before we talk about anything else, though." He took her hands. "There's something I want to ask you." His smile widened to a heart-wrenching grin. "I've been thinking about this for a couple of days now and I really feel it's the right thing to do."

Oh no. He couldn't.

No.

No matter how much she cared for him, this was wrong for both of them. Jenny's words had driven the point home. Ty would never be happy with her for a wife. He deserved someone who could be the kind of life partner he deserved.

And it wasn't her.

She wanted to do more than just be a stay-at-home wife.

She wouldn't put either of them through that.

She backed away from him, breaking the contact of their hands. "I'm sorry, Ty." She shook her head, struggling to hold the tears back. "I can't do this."

His expression clouded for a moment, then cleared as if he'd just realized her hesitation. "Yes, you can," he insisted. "It won't be that difficult. I'll make it work if you'll just give me the chance. I promise."

Oh, God. He was going to ask her. She couldn't let him. It would only hurt them both in the long run.

He reached for her hand again. "No." She stumbled back a couple more steps. "Don't." He stilled, confused, concerned. "I can't do this," she explained, hysteria rising in her voice. "I can't say yes. Please don't ask me to marry you, Ty, because I can't."

The look on his face almost undid her. She shook her head, hot tears streaming down her cheeks. "I can't marry you," she repeated, her voice now scarcely above a whisper. Before he could say anything she ran out of the barn without looking back.

It was the best thing for both of them. When he'd had a chance to think about it he'd realize it, too.

Chapter Thirteen

Stunned, Dex stared after Leanne. Marry him? She'd thought he was going to ask her to marry him? His intent had been to coax her into agreeing to his new plan for blasting her dude ranch into success. A friend of his in the travel business had agreed to include Leanne on his Web site. Dex had also managed to get a fantastic deal on furnishings for the guest cabins, furnishing he'd already taken the liberty of ordering.

Everything was set. All he'd had to do was talk Leanne into it.

I can't marry you.

Something shifted close to his heart and he felt an odd sense of panic. He shook his head, confused by his reaction to her totally unexpected words.

He'd had no intention of asking her to marry him.

Had he?

The idea was preposterous.

Wasn't it?

Need, desire and an overwhelming urge to reclaim what was his only added to his mushrooming confusion. He'd made her his, on a physical level at least.

Had those intense feelings somehow spilled over to something more?

Whatever it was, he had to do something. He couldn't just let her go.

Not like this.

There had to be a way to figure this out.

To make it right somehow.

Dex strode out of the barn and across the yard only to see the dust flying behind her as she sped away in her old truck.

Defeat weighed heavily on his shoulders. He'd done this all wrong. A sinking feeling accompanied the realization that he couldn't see any way to undo the damage. He'd messed up everything.

"She just needs some time."

Dex turned slowly to face his grandmother. "You don't understand…" He attempted to explain but couldn't find the right words. The weight on his shoulders suddenly dropped to his chest.

That steady, knowing gaze held his when he wanted to look away. "Yes, I do," she told him, her voice as steady as her gaze. "I'd just gotten out of my car when Leanne came flying out of that barn."

"She thought I was going to ask her to marry me," Dex admitted. He tried to drag a breath into his lungs, but the effort proved too monumental. "She said she can't marry me…but I…" He shook his head, uncertain of what to say or do. "She doesn't understand."

Grandmother Cooper patted his arm. "Come help me with my packages and I'll explain a few things to you."

Numbly, he followed her. She opened the back door of her car and hesitated. "We'd always thought it would happen, you know. Ty always..." She looked away a moment, as if catching herself before she said too much. "Ty and Leanne always seemed so close, such good friends. It was perfect. The ranches would be combined finally." She shrugged. "But the sparks just didn't come. The relationship never went beyond friends." Her gaze came back to rest upon his. "Not until now...until *you* came home."

Another surge of emotion shook him. She did know. "I didn't mean for it to happen. I don't even understand how it happened." He stared directly into the eyes analyzing him so closely. "I didn't come here to hurt anyone."

She nodded once. "I'm sure you'll explain everything when you're ready, but this isn't about how your being here came about. This is about Leanne. The whole town, the family, for that matter, thinks there's going to be a wedding. Whatever it takes, I know you'll make this right."

He massaged his forehead, only now aware that a piercing pain had begun there. "I will."

She reached into the back seat of her vehicle and retrieved a bag. "Leanne has been determined to make her father's dream come true for three years now. She's fiercely independent. She wants to make it on her own. Her mother's poor health is all that's stopped her." Grandmother Cooper thought for a moment before she spoke again. "It won't be easy to make her see that there's more to life than that ranch. That she doesn't have to be afraid of going out on a limb emotionally." She thrust the bag she held at Dex. "She has to understand that falling in love with you won't change who she is. This sudden about-face in what she's believed, what she's felt for years, has her running scared."

Dex laughed, a sound that held no humor. "I'm pretty damned scared myself. I've never been this confused before." He scrubbed his free hand over his face and sighed wearily. "I can't change what I've done. I wouldn't change any of it if I could," he said with complete conviction. "I know it's not going to be easy to make it right, but I'll face the consequences of my actions."

"Do I hear another 'but' in there?" she prodded, somehow reading the hesitation he'd hoped to conceal.

"But what if she refuses to understand why I've been less than honest?"

Grandmother Cooper passed another shopping bag to him, then smiled, her expression sage. "I have a feeling you haven't been yourself lately, son. Maybe you need to think long and hard about the future and what you really want...*who* you really want in it. You'll never straighten out this situation until you know what it is *you* want."

She was right. He had some thinking to do. Decisions to make. Damage to undo.

Soon, Ty had said.

Well, soon was today.

A BAG OF GROCERIES in one arm, Leanne wiped her eyes with her free hand and took a couple of deep breaths before she faced her mother. The last thing she wanted to do was worry her. Leanne closed her eyes and pushed all thoughts of Ty away. Her heart ached unbearably. But she'd done the right thing. She knew she had. She couldn't possibly marry him. It would be a mistake.

It had all happened too fast. One month ago she and Ty had been nothing more than friends, close friends, but friends nonetheless. Then out of the blue things got all confused, turned upside down. It had started the day she picked him up from the airport. She remembered clearly feeling that uncharacteristic pull of attraction. He'd been behaving strangely as well, she'd noticed. Nothing about him felt the same. Leanne frowned. Between the changes in Ty, her own crazy hormones and the pressure from the whole community to get them together, it was no wonder they'd fallen into each other's arms.

They'd simply done what everyone had wanted all along. She took another deep breath. Though she loved him, there was no doubt about that, it didn't change the fact that she and Ty weren't right for each other. She obviously didn't love him the way she should or she wouldn't be having these second thoughts. She didn't want to be known only as Mrs. Ty Cooper. She closed her eyes and shook her head at that untruth. She did love him…completely. She wanted him desperately. Would like nothing more than to spend the rest of her life with him, making love the way they had this week. She just wasn't willing to sacrifice who she was—who she wanted to be—in order to make it happen.

Besides Ty hadn't said one thing about being in love with her. Though she could tell that he cared for her, that was clear. Had she given him the opportunity to propose, would he regret it when the heady rush of lust wore off? This wild attraction had come on so suddenly, so unexpectedly…putting much stock into it was simply too scary. What if it was only a passing fancy?

What if they both woke up six months down the road and realized they'd made a terrible mistake?

She couldn't take that chance.

Gathering her composure, she forced a smile and opened the door.

"I'm back," she called as she stepped into the quiet house. She frowned when a soft sound snagged her attention. Scanning the room, her heart dropped into her stomach when her gaze landed on her mother huddled on the couch sobbing.

The sack of groceries hit the floor. "Mama!" She fell to her knees next to the couch. "What's wrong? Did you hear from the doctor?"

Joanna looked up, her face damp with tears. She flung her arms around her daughter and hugged her tight. "Everything's going to be all right." Another sob wracked her frail form. "She called."

Leanne drew back, her own tears flowing now. "Tell me what she said." She hated that she'd missed that call. She forced away the thoughts of Ty that tried to surface.

Joanna shook her head. "It's so simple. My thyroid stopped working."

Confusion lined Leanne's brow. "But you had tests for that."

Her mother nodded. "I know. It's called a silent thyroid. It slows down, then completely stops, causing everything else to go haywire. The strange thing is it's very difficult to diagnose. The usual blood tests won't catch it, everything continues to appear normal.''

"What does this mean? What can be done about it?" Leanne wanted to be thrilled, but she needed to know for sure that it could be fixed.

"Dr. Baker brought the medicine out to me a few minutes ago." She nodded to the red-and-white striped bag on the sofa table. "I'll be taking a stimulant until it starts to work on its own again. He'll monitor the situation from here on out. He said I should see a noticeable difference right away."

Leanne sagged with relief. "Thank God," she murmured.

"And Ty," Joanna added. "He's a fine man, Leanne."

She could only nod. Tears had already sprung up to the point of spilling past her lashes.

"Whatever you do, don't ever let him go."

The ache in her chest sharpened, making it impossible to breathe and at the same time impossible not to weep.

Too late, she cried silently. *Too late.*

DEX HAD DONE just as his grandmother suggested, he'd thought long and hard about his future. He'd spent most of the afternoon walking the floor of his room, studying the picture of his parents, and considering all that he'd learned since coming to Montana. The truth had rattled him just a little.

These people were family to him, there was no denying that. He wanted them to be a part of his life even after he went back to Atlanta.

He just didn't know how he was going to break the

truth to any of them. His grandmother already knew, had known practically from the beginning. He sat down on the edge of the bed and contemplated the best course of action. Should he just wait until they were gathered around the dinner table and make an announcement? He shook his head. No, that would be too abrupt. A family meeting? The Montgomerys were famous for family meetings.

Dex wondered vaguely how Ty was making out at this point. Dex would have to inform him right away that he'd let the cat out of the bag, so to speak. He felt fairly confident that the Coopers would want to call Ty immediately to see that he was all right. Dex tried not to consider how his Atlanta family was going to take all this. It wouldn't be pleasant. Though Dex still knew little about what had precipitated this break between their families, he had a feeling that there was some really bad blood, otherwise there would have been no need for the secrecy all these years.

Maybe before he did anything else he would ask his grandmother to tell him the whole story. He knew from what Ty had told him and from Grandfather Montgomery's bluntness about his disappointment in his son's marriage, that the couple's coming together had not been accepted—at least not by the Montgomerys. But it went deeper than that.

Dex would have to have the answers before he came clean with the rest of the family.

But before he did anything else, he had to make things right with Leanne. He would not put her through any more unnecessary grief. She was his first order of business.

When he stood it took a moment to steady himself as memories and sensations toppled one over the other inside him. He couldn't imagine never being able to touch her again, never being able to kiss those sweet lips.

But did these feelings translate into the kind of love that led to a lifetime commitment? The kind of commitment Leanne deserved? Dex exhaled a heavy breath. He didn't know. He'd never been in love before, but every instinct told him that this was it. There were plenty of facts to go along with the instinct, too. Like the fact that he couldn't sleep or eat. And the fact that his every thought related to, began or ended with her.

Now he only had to figure out how he was going to make this right, make it work out, when she didn't even know who he was. He could just imagine the betrayal she would feel when she learned the truth. He tamped down the outright fear that accompanied that thought.

No point in putting off the inevitable. He had to do this. He had to do it now.

Dex picked up the ever-present, cursed hat from the dresser. That automatic action drew him up short. He almost laughed. Damn if he wasn't turning into a cowboy after all. Shaking his head he headed downstairs. Maybe, in time, she would forgive him for lying to her, misleading her and taking her innocence. Hell, he wasn't even sure he could forgive himself.

The twins sat on the last tread at the bottom of the staircase. "Excuse me, gentlemen," he said playfully. "I hope I don't need a special password to be allowed through."

The boys shook their heads simultaneously. "You need money," one said, then held out his hand. "Lotsa money."

Dex frowned, trying to decide which was which. "Money, huh?"

"Yep," the other one said. "Angelica says we gotta give the new baby all our toys. We need money to buy new ones."

A grin eased across Dex's face. That was just like Angelica. Already planning a strategy so she didn't have to sacrifice for the new baby. Dex decided then and there that the little girl would make a great businesswoman when she grew up. "She told you that, huh?"

The boys nodded.

"Well," Dex said with finality. "You boys tell Angelica that if she insists on you giving the new baby all your toys that your Uncle De—Ty will just have to buy you new ones."

Their eyes went round. The two munchkins jumped up and raced away amid a chorus of yippees!

Dex took the last couple of steps and headed for the door. Kids. That was another thing he had to factor into his future. He paused, hand on the doorknob. Had he really just thought that? This place had obviously gotten to him even more than he'd realized.

"Do you have a minute, son?"

Dex turned to find his grandfather in the entry hall behind him. He looked solemn or weary, or maybe both. "Sure." Dex took the three steps that separated them.

Grandfather Cooper stared at the floor for a time, just long enough to make Dex uneasy. "I've been doing a lot of thinking since you got back from Chicago.''

Dex went on instant alert. Had his grandmother told her husband who Dex really was?

He looked up at Dex then. "Since you've been back there's been times when you seemed almost like a stranger." He shrugged. "I know it sounds funny, but you just haven't acted like the Ty we know."

"I...I've been under a lot of stress," Dex offered hesitantly. He didn't want it to go down like this.

His grandfather nodded. "I know. And I feel like part of that is my fault."

Dex frowned. He opened his mouth to deny the assertion, but fell silent in anticipation of the older man's next words.

Grandfather Cooper released a breath wrought with anxiety. "I've made some mistakes in my life. Plenty." He shook his head. "But there are some I'm more ashamed of than others." He leveled that uncertain gaze on Dex's once more. "Your behavior the past few weeks has made me think how different things might have been if certain circumstances had been different. Made me wonder what I'd missed."

Another of those unfamiliar emotions, helplessness, washed over Dex.

That same helplessness was reflected in the older man's eyes. "I know I'm not making any sense, but it's been on my mind and I had to tell you how I feel. I should never have allowed anything to get in the way of what was right."

It made perfect sense to Dex. His grandfather regretted that the boys had been separated. Dex's un-Ty-like behavior had made him think and wonder about how the other twin, the one they'd given up, had turned out.

Grandfather Cooper's eyes brightened with emotion. "I just wish things had been different, that's all. We didn't want it this way. But, under the circumstances, it was the only way. Too much water had gone under the bridge."

Dex nodded. The bitterness he would have expected to feel a few weeks ago never appeared. He slung an arm around his grandfather's slumped shoulders. "Me, too."

His grandfather looked at him. "You're a good man, Ty. Like your father."

Dex wanted to thank him for saying so, even if he wasn't Ty, but if he spoke right now he would never be able to hold back the emotions pounding against his shaky facade of calm. Instead, he nodded again. There was so much that needed to be said, that needed to be done. He needed so many answers.

But not now. He had to work things out with Leanne first.

Distress claimed the older man's features. He opened his mouth to speak, but only uttered a gasping sound. He clutched at his chest, then crumpled in Dex's arms.

Startled, Dex lowered his grandfather to the floor. He recognized the signs instantly. A cold, hard knot of fear formed in his stomach. A cardiac episode. His grandfather gasping for breath, Dex ripped the man's shirt open and jerked it loose from his jeans.

Years of training overriding his fear, Dex shouted, "I need some help in here!" He checked his grandfather's carotid pulse. Thready, but there. Dex said a silent prayer of thanks, his finger still gauging the pitifully weak beat.

"Stay calm," Dex assured the older man. "Everything's going to be fine." God he hoped he was right. His grandfather struggled to drag air into his lungs. "I want you to try to relax. Don't be afraid. I'm here. I won't let anything happen to you." Another promise he hoped he could keep.

"Wayne!" Grandmother Cooper fell to her knees next to her husband.

Brenda and Jenny flocked around her.

"Call 911," Dex commanded. "Tell them—"

No pulse.

Dex swore. He leaned down, putting his cheek close to the man's mouth. He wasn't breathing. "Now!" Dex shouted when no one moved to make the call. He gave his grandfather two puffs of air and watched the fall of his chest as the air rushed out through his open mouth. Still no pulse.

"What's happening?" Grandmother Cooper cried.

Dex moved into position to do chest compressions. "Is he on any medication?"

His grandmother shook her head, fear shining in her eyes.

"Any heart problems?" One, two, three, he counted silently.

"No," she wailed. "What's happening?"

Another two puffs of air…more compressions. Ignoring the sounds and faces around him, Dex repeated the routine again and then again. He paused, watched for spontaneous breathing and checked the carotid pulse.

Faint, but it was back.

Thank God.

"Is he having a heart attack?" Jenny asked, her arms around the older woman now.

"He can't be having a heart attack," Grandmother Cooper argued, panic rising in her voice. "He doesn't have any heart problems."

Dex leveled the calmest gaze he could manage on his grandmother, his finger resting lightly on the weak pulse that told him his grandfather was hanging on…just barely. "We need help *fast*."

No further explanation was needed.

Brenda thrust the telephone at Dex. "She wants to talk to you," she said between sobs.

Dex took the phone.

"I'm going to get Chad and Court," Brenda called, near hysteria herself, as she rushed out the front door, leaving it standing wide open.

"Seventy-eight-year-old white male. Excellent physical condition, non-smoker, no history of cardiac disease, no meds," Dex told the 911 operator. "Complete cardiopulmonary arrest, but I have a faint rhythm going again. Pulse is thready. No way to gauge BP. What's your ETA?"

Fifteen minutes.

Dex breathed a curse. "Just hurry."

The pulse faded once more.

Dammit. "I've lost him again. Tell the EMT we're going to need full advanced cardiac life support. We need it *stat!*"

Dex allowed the phone to drop to the floor as he bent forward and forced another couple of quick breaths of life-giving oxygen into his grandfather's lungs. While he performed another set of chest compressions Jenny picked up the receiver and answered any other questions the operator had.

Dex leaned forward to issue another breath. "Don't you die on me," he murmured. "We have things to settle."

Chapter Fourteen

By the time the ambulance arrived, Dex had again established and maintained a weak, but spontaneous rhythm. For the moment his grandfather was holding his own. Dex was exhausted and weak with relief when he finally relinquished care to the EMTs.

The rest of the family stood in a semi-circle around Dex, too stunned or too worried to utter the questions clear on their faces. Angelica and the twins sobbed in their mothers' arms.

Dex's entire body started to shake with the receding adrenaline. He'd forgotten how frightening a moment like this could be. He'd kept his grandfather alive long enough for prepared help to arrive. The likelihood of his survival had he not had immediate and expert attention would have been extremely slim.

Aboard the ambulance, one EMT hovered over his grandfather's gurney, monitoring his vitals and adjusting the intravenous flow, the other assisted Grandmother Cooper inside. Once she was settled next to her husband, the young man turned to Dex. "You did a great job, Mr. Cooper."

Doctor Montgomery, Dex corrected silently. He

was Dr. Montgomery, but he was too uncertain of his voice at this point to speak. What was he thinking? He couldn't have said that anyway.

Frowning thoughtfully, the man slammed the rear doors, closing off the worried face of Dex's grandmother. He hesitated before going to the cab. "Have you had medical training?" He studied Dex speculatively. "You seemed to know a whole lot more than your average CPR-certified civilian."

Dex couldn't answer. He was too emotionally drained to even attempt a response.

Everyone watched in expectant anticipation of some sort of plausible excuse for what they'd just witnessed first-hand.

The guy shrugged. "Too many episodes of *ER,* I guess." He clapped Dex on the shoulder. "We're taking him to Mercy. He's stable, so don't drive like a bat out of hell getting the rest of the family there."

Sirens blaring, lights flashing, the ambulance sped down the long drive, a cloud of dust billowing in its wake.

"Chad, you take Jenny, Brenda and the kids in the minivan." Court glanced at Dex, his expression as well as his tone brooking no argument. "Ty and I'll come in the truck."

Jenny straggled behind, reluctant to drag her gaze from Dex. He remembered the day she'd hugged him so fiercely and shared her life-altering news. The hurt and confusion was clear in her eyes now. Hurt Dex had put there. He'd lied to them all, and though they were too concerned about their grandfather at the moment to dwell on the matter, they knew something was very wrong.

Dex met Court's suspicious glare. "I know you want answers," he said, struggling for calm. "But now is not the time. We need to get to that hospital."

"You think I don't know that?" his brother demanded. "Let's go."

Neither of them spoke during the seemingly endless trip to Bozeman. Dex thanked God again for the emergency medical station in Rolling Bend. He wasn't sure he could have kept his grandfather going long enough for help to arrive all the way from Bozeman.

As they entered the city limits, Court finally broke the silence. "Who are you?"

Dex had known that was coming. He'd braced himself, considered his response. Still, he wasn't fully prepared for the question when it came. He took a heavy breath. Maybe it wasn't the question he wasn't ready for, maybe it was the anger and accusation he heard in Court's voice. Whichever it was, it struck a painful chord deep in Dex's chest.

For one long moment as he stared out at the traffic before them, Dex considered lying...keeping up the ruse. But it wouldn't be right. It hadn't been right from the beginning. He and Ty had made a mistake.

A mistake that would hurt the people they both cared about most.

Dex closed his eyes for a second to block the painful images of his grandfather...of Leanne. And then of the way Jenny had looked at him.

It was time to face the reality of what he'd done.

"My name is Dex Montgomery."

There was no way to miss Court's reaction. He knew the name. Ty had been a Montgomery until the

Coopers had legally adopted him. The whole Cooper family knew who Charles Dexter Montgomery, Junior, was. He was Ty's father.

Dex's father.

Court glanced at him with something resembling uncertainty. "Where's Ty?"

"He's in Atlanta with my...with his other grandparents."

Court looked both ways at the intersection then sped through the red light to keep up with the ambulance. He took a left, then parked in the lot designated as E.R. parking.

He shut the engine off and looked at Dex before getting out. "I don't know how this can be possible. We thought..." Court shook his head. "But one thing I do know is that you lied to us." He shook his head. "I knew something was wrong but I never would have believed this. You had to know how this would affect all of us. What were you thinking? What was Ty thinking?"

Dex didn't blink under that hard stare. "We weren't."

Court clenched his jaw. He blinked then, but not before Dex saw the renewed anger in his eyes. "Why didn't you just tell us who you were?" he accused.

"We can talk about this later. Right now we have something much more important to do."

Court nodded. "You're right." He hesitated once more before getting out. "Later, I want the whole story. And I want to talk to my brother."

Dex followed Court through the automatic doors that slid open to admit them into the E.R. Court's words rang in his ears. *I want to talk to my brother.*

That was the bottom line. Ty was Court's brother, not Dex.

LEANNE'S TRUCK squealed to a stop in the parking lot outside the emergency room entrance of Mercy Hospital. She slammed the old gear shift into Park and burst out of her truck. Mr. Cooper'd had a heart attack according to Agnes Washburn, whose nephew worked as a paramedic in Rolling Bend.

Her heart pounding, she raced toward the entrance. Ty needed her. She had to be there for him. Nothing else mattered at the moment. She blinked back a fresh wave of tears. If his grandfather died... No! She would not think that way. Mr. Cooper had to be all right.

"Leanne?"

She stopped abruptly and looked around to find who'd spoken. Craig Washburn stood a few feet away, smoking a cigarette. Though she hadn't run into Craig in years, they had gone to school together, and he really hadn't changed much. His blue uniform was rumpled and he looked tired. A long shift, she supposed. He flipped the butt of his cigarette away and started in her direction.

"You here about Mr. Cooper?"

She nodded. "How is he?"

Craig blew out a mighty breath. "Very lucky."

Leanne frowned. "Lucky?"

"He's stable. According to the doc on call, if Ty hadn't done what he did his grandfather would have been DOA." He adopted a pointed look. "Dead on arrival."

Leanne knew what he meant. She moistened her lips. "Ty was able to help him?"

Craig made a sound, not quite a laugh. "Help him? Heck, he kept the old man alive." Craig shook his head. "I don't know where he took his training, but he not only performed the necessary CPR, he told us exactly what he needed. We were able to confirm medical orders from the doc on call while en route, based on the details Ty gave us over the phone."

An emotion akin to fear stole into Leanne's heart. She shook her head. "Ty's never had any medical training."

Craig shook another cigarette out of the pack he kept in his breast pocket. "That may be, but I know what I saw with my own eyes, what I heard with my own ears. I'm telling you the guy knows his stuff. Damned if he didn't sound and act just like a doctor." He flicked his lighter and inhaled deeply, then blew out a puff of gray smoke. "I've worked with enough of 'em to know one when I hear one. The way he started barking orders to us the second we arrived." Craig shrugged. "I'm just telling you how it happened." He angled his head toward the E.R. entrance. "The whole family's in there looking at him as if he's from outer space."

Every ounce of warmth in her body drained clean out of Leanne. Angelica's words about Ty having been abducted by aliens echoed in her mind. The dozens of small things she'd ignored over the past few weeks all flickered across her mind's eye. The way he talked...the way he moved. Her heart thundered in her chest. The way he touched her...her response to his touch.

Her body began to shake uncontrollably as the ice slowly slid through her veins. Now she knew why he'd behaved so strangely since coming back from Chicago...Ty wasn't himself.

He was someone else.

And whoever he was, he'd made her fall in love with him...he'd made love to her.

Craig steadied her when she would have dropped like a rock onto the sidewalk. "You all right, Leanne? Maybe you should come in and sit down. You look like you've just seen a ghost."

No ghost, she was too weak to protest, an impostor.

DEX STOOD on one side of the E.R. waiting room, which was empty except for the rest of the Cooper family, who were gathered on the opposite side as if they were afraid to get too close to him.

He forced himself not to dwell on what they clearly thought about him now. While he had relayed the details to the physician on call, Court had apparently filled the rest of the family in on who Dex really was. The suspicious looks cast his way by one member of the Cooper clan after the other made him want to lash out, to tell them that it wasn't his fault. He and Ty had done the only thing they could considering their circumstances.

He closed his eyes and mentally blocked out how he thought Leanne would react when she learned the truth. She would be hurt worst of all.

Dex ran a hand through his hair. They all hated him now and he couldn't blame any of them. He'd lied to them. Used them for his own personal gain.

He had to call Ty. But he'd put off making that

call until he had further word on his grandfather's condition. He didn't want to upset him unnecessarily.

The double doors that boasted Authorized Personnel Only suddenly opened. Grandmother Cooper, looking far too weary, emerged. The rest of the family crowded around her, launching a barrage of questions the moment the automatic doors slowly began to close behind her.

Dex kept his distance. He was an outsider. He might as well acknowledge his new standing with the other half of his family.

"Your grandfather is stable and conscious. He's resting comfortably now," she announced. Her words were punctuated by a collective sigh of relief. "They're going to keep him a couple of days to perform a few tests to assess any damage done by the heart attack and to determine the best way to make sure it doesn't happen again."

Tears and hugs filled the silence that followed. Dex watched, so relieved that his grandfather was going to be all right that he couldn't muster up any negative emotion regarding his new standing. He closed his eyes and silently thanked God, something he'd been doing a lot of lately.

He opened his eyes just in time to find his grandmother looking directly at him. She made her way through the loved ones gathered around her and walked straight up to him.

Dex squared his shoulders and braced himself for further rejection.

"I don't know quite what to say," she murmured, her voice strained. She blinked furiously, futilely attempting to hold back the tears spilling down her cheeks.

Dex wanted to tell her he was sorry, to beg her not to say anything. He wasn't sure his heart could take any more. He'd never felt this close to complete and utter desolation. But he couldn't, he couldn't say anything. They were right, he was wrong. He'd made a mistake.

She lifted her chin and stared straight at him. "There is nothing I can say, nothing I can do to show you how very grateful I am for what you did today." Her voice cracked just a little on the last word. "Despite knowing the personal repercussions of your actions, you saved my husband's life," she whispered. "You have no idea what that means to me. Thank you."

Dex didn't even try to stop the tears dampening his face. "I'm glad I was here to help."

She smiled. "Me, too." Grandmother Cooper hugged him close. His chest constricted. When at last she released him, she turned back to the rest of her family. "I have to get back to your grandfather soon. But first, there's something you all need to realize." She reached for Dex's hand and squeezed it. "This man saved your grandfather's life. Though we might not understand the circumstances that brought him back into our lives, the only thing we need to know is that he's family." She looked from one wary face to the other. "You treat him with the love and respect he deserves."

Dex stood very still, too uncertain...too undone even to guess what would happen next.

Jenny was the first to approach him. She smiled a

watery smile up at him. "Welcome to the family—
Dex."

She hugged him. "We're glad to have you home."

Dex trembled as his arms went around her. "Thank
you," he managed to mutter.

One by one, the entire Cooper clan hugged him,
more tears flowing. Angelica waited until next to last.
She waltzed up to Dex and extended her arms upward. "Thank you, Uncle..." She scrunched her forehead in confusion. "Uncle Tex," she finished with a
wide gap-toothed grin.

Dex felt a smile tug at his lips as he knelt in front
of her and took the hug she offered.

"Listen, whoever you are," she whispered into his
ear, "you'd better get them babies off my back. They
keep dumpin' all their ol' yucky toys in my room."

He drew back and winked at her. "Don't worry,
princess, I'm sure it'll all work out."

She scowled her five-year-old best at him before
trudging off to join her mother. Dex stood, painfully
aware that Court had not made an effort as yet.

Before he'd scarcely completed the thought, Court
took the two steps necessary to put himself within
handshaking distance. He thrust out his right hand. "I
want to thank you for what you did...Dex."

Dex accepted his hand and gave it one firm pump.
"That's not necessary." He looked the other man
straight in the eye. "He's my grandfather, too."

Court nodded solemnly. "You're right." He smiled
then. "It's good to have you in the family." He
pulled Dex into a heartfelt embrace.

When Court finally released him, he asked, "What
are you, a doctor or something?"

Dex smiled, suddenly tired all over again. "Yeah. That's what I am." For the first time since his residency, he felt exactly like a doctor.

"Leanne, we didn't even see you over there," Brenda said suddenly, looking somewhere beyond Dex.

Time lapsed into slow motion then. Dex turned to face the only woman in this world who'd ever touched him deep inside. The hurt and confusion on her pretty face slammed into him like a blow to his abdomen.

She walked straight up to him and slapped him hard. He didn't blink, instead he allowed the sting to reverberate all the way to his heart. He deserved whatever she felt compelled to throw his way.

"I can't believe you lied to me." She shook her head slowly from side to side. "How could you pretend to be Ty...and do what you did?"

Dex felt unsteady on his feet. He'd never experienced this level of regret or pain before. "I didn't mean to hurt you. I only came here to get to know the other half of my family." He gestured vaguely. "It just happened," he explained softly.

She glowered at him, her fists clenched at her sides. "Were you just slumming, Doctor? Surely you didn't come here to stay?"

He closed his eyes against the anguish staring back at him...against the hurt throbbing in his chest.

"Answer me, dammit!" she demanded. "Did you come here to stay?"

It took all the courage he could dredge up to open his eyes to her again. He shook his head, the gesture hardly more than a tic. "No."

The new flash of pain that flickered in those blue eyes ripped the heart right out of his chest.

"What was I?" she demanded, her voice faltering. "The entertainment?"

"Leanne, I—"

She took two stumbling steps backward, as if the mere sound of his voice had propelled her. "It doesn't matter. Just go back to wherever you came from and stay away from me."

She left him standing there, knowing for the first time in his life how it felt to have a broken heart.

"Dex."

He felt his grandmother's hand on his arm; slowly he turned to face her.

"You have to give her some more time," she offered kindly. "She feels betrayed."

He released a shaky breath. "I don't think there'll ever be enough time."

Grandmother Cooper took his hand in hers. "Come over here and sit down with me for a moment. We need to talk." She sent a pointed look across the waiting room.

"Let's go down to the cafeteria and get some coffee," Chad suggested a little more loudly than necessary.

The rest of the family looked startled for a moment, then realized what was going on. Sounds of agreement rumbled through the group.

"The babies can't have coffee, can they, daddy?" Angelica announced as her father led her away.

Dex heard the patience in Chad's voice as he answered the princess. Dex found himself wondering what it would be like to have a child of his own, one completely unlike the princess, of course.

God, he had lost it.

Grandmother Cooper settled into a blue molded plastic chair and gestured to the one beside her. "There are a few things you need to think about before this goes any further."

Dex wasn't sure if he was up to this talk right now, but she appeared intent on giving it to him. "I'm listening."

"The history between the Montgomerys and the Coopers goes back a long ways. Back to when your father and mother were just children." She sighed, her gaze taking on that distant look he'd seen before when she talked about the past. "They were so different from us. They didn't want their Chuck being with Tara." She shook her head. "Your Grandfather Montgomery was president of the Rolling Bend Bank. He turned us down for a loan during a bad time. We barely survived. There were a lot of hard feelings."

Dex listened, a frown etching its way across his brow. It was hard to believe this whole cover-up went that far back. He found it even harder to believe his grandfather could have been so heartless. His lips formed a grim line. No, he didn't. If the Coopers were having a bad time of it and appeared to be a credit risk, he would have turned them down flat. It wouldn't have been personal, just business. Dex had made those same kinds of decisions himself. How could he have been so wrong? How could his grandfather have been so wrong?

"Anyway, the Montgomerys moved down to Atlanta when your father was still a boy. They knew even then that he loved our Tara. But they refused to allow it.'' She paused, a tiny smile playing about her lips. ''Then, years later, when they were all grown up, Tara and your father met again.'' She looked directly at Dex then. ''Completely by accident. Before any of us knew what was happening, they'd married. The Montgomerys would have none of it. Your Grandfather Montgomery threatened to disown your father if he didn't annul the marriage and return to Atlanta immediately. Of course, Chuck wouldn't do it. The next thing we knew, you boys were on the way.''

Tears glistened in her eyes. ''When you were only three months old...we lost them.'' She swiped at the tears determined to fall. ''That's when things went to hell in a handbasket.''

Dex couldn't speak, emotion had him by the throat. He could only sit there and wait for her to continue.

''The Montgomerys were determined to have the babies. We were just as determined to keep the two of you.'' She closed her eyes, visibly grappling for composure.

He knew there was something he should say or do, but the images her words evoked held him in a firm grip of silence.

''The legal battle went on for weeks, then months. Finally some hare-brained judge decided to do what he called the only fair thing to do, give one baby to us, one to them.'' She sighed again. ''Because of the awful feud between the two families, the judge further ordered that there would be no communication between us unless it was a medical emergency until we learned to get along. By the time we got around to thinking how wrong the whole thing was, too much time had passed. It didn't seem right to disrupt your lives at that point."

Dex felt an odd sense of relief at the realization that his Grandfather Montgomery hadn't master-minded that whole plot.

Grandmother Cooper's gaze locked with his once more. "There have been far too many betrayals and lies in this family already," she said in earnest. "It's time we made this whole mess right."

"How do we do that?" Dex felt hopeless all over again.

"We have to call Ty and tell him what's happened. We have to find a way to bury the hatchet with the Montgomerys."

Dex lifted a skeptical brow. "After the way my grandfather disowned my father, I'm not sure I can make that happen," he said, feeling suddenly, completely empty.

"Your grandfather was hurting, Dex," she argued. "I'd be the last person on the earth to take his side, but the one thing I know for certain is how much he and your grandmother loved your father. They were hurt and lashed out."

Dex shook his head. "That still doesn't excuse his actions." Anger ignited, replacing the emptiness. "There's no excuse for that."

"You're right. It was the wrong thing to do, com-pletely inexcusable." She placed her hand over his. "But I want you to think about the heavy price your grandparents have had to pay for that mistake."

Dex stilled at her words.

"Your father, their only child, died without their

being able to make amends with him.'' A lone tear trekked down her pale cheek. "There is no greater pain than the loss of a child, especially if that child is uncertain about how much you love him. I know, because I lost Tara. Your Grandfather Montgomery never got to make things right with his son.''

Dex closed his eyes to block the sting of tears.

"I think they've paid enough.''

Chapter Fifteen

Dex wasn't exactly sure how long he'd sat in the deserted cafeteria before he made a decision, but it had been a considerable length of time. The fact that the rest of the Cooper clan, as well as the lunch crowd, had long since dispersed, made him reasonably sure that he'd been there two or three hours.

Long enough to know what he had to do. One way or another he had to make things right with Leanne. He would not leave Montana with this chasm between them. Right now, though, he couldn't do anything about that. He had to give her time to come to terms with what she'd learned about him today. Just as he'd had to accept this other part of who he was.

He would give her a few days, then he'd make her listen to reason. He was too good a negotiator even to think about defeat. Somehow he'd work this out.

But today, right now, he decided as he stood, he had a couple of things that he needed to attend to. As he exited the cafeteria he thought about all that his grandmother had told him. Once he'd assured her that he would call Ty, he'd come down here to think things through. He'd needed a little time to formulate a plan. And he'd done that.

Dex took the elevator back to the third floor, where his Grandfather Cooper had been admitted into the intensive care unit. At the nurses' desk, he paused to speak with the doctor who'd just made his afternoon rounds.

"Excuse me, Doctor…" Dex checked his nametag, "…Louden, I'm Dr. Montgomery. I'm here with the Coopers."

Dr. Louden looked up from the notes he'd been in the process of adding to a chart. "Yes." He extended his hand, which Dex promptly shook. "Chad Cooper went to school with my younger sister. I'm glad Mr. Cooper is doing well. Is there anything I can do for you, Dr. Montgomery?"

"Do you have a conference room available that I could use to consult with some of my colleagues in Atlanta?"

He nodded. "Certainly. It's on the first floor. Stop at the information desk. I'll call down and have someone waiting to show you the way."

"Thank you."

Less than ten minutes later Dex stood alone at a polished mahogany conference table, waiting for his personal secretary to put him through to the man she thought to be Dex Montgomery.

"Ty, it's me, Dex."

"Hey, what's going on there?"

Dex frowned. Ty sounded strange. Dex dreaded giving him this news. "I'm afraid Grandfather Cooper has had a heart attack."

"How—?"

"He's all right," Dex cut in, reassuring his brother. "We got him to the hospital and he's in stable condition."

"Are you sure—" his voice broke "—he's all right?"

Dex explained each procedure performed on his grandfather. Then the tests to assess his condition and the results. Finally he convinced Ty that he was stable and in no immediate danger. "He's strong, Ty. And the family's here with him."

"I'll be on the next flight out," Ty insisted, his voice strained with worry.

"I figured you would." Dex paused. "But we need to straighten out some things first."

"I know," Ty told him. "All hell broke out here this morning. I was getting ready to call you."

Dex frowned. "What's happened?"

A heavy sigh sounded on the other end of the line. "Bridget figured out I wasn't you. She announced it in front of the whole hospital board, including the Montgomerys."

"Damn." This was definitely not good.

"Grandfather Montgomery didn't take it well. He thinks I came here for the money." He fell silent for a long moment. "And he wanted to know what I'd done with you."

Dex hissed a curse. "Where is he now?"

"In a closed-door meeting with Bridget. They're probably trying to figure out how to protect themselves from me."

Fury boiled up inside Dex. Money. It was always the bottom line. "I'll talk to him."

"There's something else we have to settle."

As Dex listened, Ty explained about a children's center he wanted to help Jessica Stovall build. It would mean a lot to her as well as the children of Atlanta. It sounded good to Dex. Then Ty told him about the possible embezzlements and the notations on the accounts.

"We'll fund the center," Dex told him without hesitation. It was past time the Montgomerys started giving something back. "I don't care what Grandfather said, you're part Montgomery, just like I'm part Cooper. I'll make good on whatever you promised the hospital."

"Thanks, man." Ty sounded relieved. "What about Bridget? She was pretty upset about using those two accounts I mentioned for the hospital fund."

Dex hesitated. "B & B," he said more to himself than Ty as he drummed his fingers on the conference table. "Dammit, I think I know what it stands for. The little backstabber," Dex growled. It made perfect sense…Bridget's Bonus…B & B. "She's skimming bonus money for herself from our accounts and we were too blind to see it."

Ty made a sound of agreement.

"I'll take care of her," Dex assured him. "Now, tell me, Ty. Did I hear a hint of something extra personal between you and this Dr. Stovall?"

"Yeah, but it's not going to happen." Sadness weighted his tone.

"Sorry." Dex knew how that felt. It looked as if they were both in the same boat where their love lives were concerned. "Listen, there's something else," Dex said, dreading this part too. "The company you met with in Chicago turned your proposal down. But I have an idea.''

"I've already got a plan,'' Ty said, more enthusiastically than Dex would have expected. "In Mom's letters she talked about raising leaner—''

"Beef,'' Dex finished with a grin. He'd come up with the same idea after seeing the picture of her receiving the nutrition award. Obviously Ty had been doing the same investigating into the past that Dex had done. "We'll need more land—''

"And I'll have to invest in different feed—''

"The Watley ranch will be perfect,'' Dex said. "We can lease the rest of the grazing land and it'll benefit the Watleys as well as us.'' Had he just said *we?*

During the pause that followed Dex realized that they had been finishing each other's sentences. Great minds think alike, he mused.

"You said *we'll* need more land. Are you planning to stay there?'' Ty wanted to know.

Dex considered that question, really considered it. Yes, he had every intention of making this his second home. "Not permanently. But I'll provide the money for the venture. You can run the day-to-day operations.''

"I don't want Montgomery money,'' Ty said tightly.

Dex restrained a sigh. "Listen, Ty, I don't give a damn what my grandfather said. We're brothers, and if I want to be partners with you, that's my choice. The Coopers are my family, too.''

When Ty remained silent, Dex said, "We can discuss it some more when you get here. Now, let me speak to Grandfather. Get him and Bridget in there and put me on speaker phone.''

Dex listened as Ty buzzed his grandfather and waited.

''What the hell do you want?'' Grandfather Montgomery thundered.

''Dex is on the phone,'' Ty said stiffly.

''Dex! Is that you, son?''

A surge of emotion made speech impossible for one long beat. ''Yes,'' he finally said. ''I'm here.''

''What the Sam Hill is going on here?'' the old man demanded. ''I don't know what kind of nonsense those *people* have put in your head, but I want you back in Atlanta ASAP!''

Fury flared anew. ''You have two options, Grandfather,'' Dex said bluntly. ''You may—''

''Dex,'' Bridget cut in sharply. ''I cannot believe you're talking to your grandfather in such a manner. What has happened to you? Who is this impostor posing as you?''

Dex settled into the closest chair and made himself comfortable. ''Bridget—''

''Dex, darling,'' she purred. ''How could you do this to us?''

''I haven't done anything yet,'' Dex said flatly.

''Please, Dex,'' Bridget hissed, ''you must admit that this whole sham is incredibly bizarre. Perhaps you need an appointment with my therapist. He's—''

''Bridget,'' Dex interrupted smoothly, ''you may leave now. You're fired.''

''Y-you can't do that!'' she stammered.

"I can and I am. And forget about taking those little bonuses with you."

Silence reigned for a few tense seconds before the sound of a slamming door announced what was no doubt her dramatic departure.

"I don't know what's gotten into you, son, but I'm warning you—" his grandfather began.

"No, Grandfather," Dex objected. "I'm warning you. On Saturday, if Grandfather Cooper is doing as well as expected, we're going to be having the mother of all barbecues at the Circle C."

"I'll be there," Ty stated for emphasis.

"By Saturday if you're not back in Atlanta—"

Dex again cut his grandfather off. "If you want me back in your life, you will accept Ty and the rest of the Coopers as family. This family feud has gone on too long. It's all or nothing, Grandfather. No compromises...no negotiations."

"How dare you issue me such an ultimatum!"

"If you're interested in remaining a part of *my* family," Dex informed him, "you'll be there on Saturday. Think about it this time. How much are you willing to lose before you realize that life is too short?"

Dex didn't give his grandfather time to argue further, he disconnected. There was nothing else to say. Ty would be flying in tonight or early tomorrow morning. Dex had done all he could from here.

Now it was time for stage two of his plan.

Winning back the woman who'd stolen his heart.

ON SATURDAY MORNING Leanne returned home from the supply store to find a huge, yellow rental truck, a moving van or something of that order parked in front of her house. Bewildered, she climbed out of her old truck and headed into the house. She could unload the horse feed later.

Inside she found her mother talking on the telephone while reviewing what appeared to be pamphlets spread out over the sofa table.

"That sounds wonderful," Joanna said. "My daughter will get back to you next week." She hung up.

Leanne hitched a thumb toward the front of the house. "What's going on? What's that truck doing here?"

"First," her mother beamed, "let me tell you about this." She thrust a colorful brochure at Leanne.

As Leanne studied the lovely travel pamphlet, her mother explained, "This is Stargazers Travel. They want to list us in their brochures and on their Web site. The president of the company thinks he can have us fully booked by next month."

Next month? "Whoa!" Leanne stared at her mother in disbelief. "How in the world do you think we can pull that off? We don't—"

"Come with me." Joanna grabbed her by the arm and tugged her through the house and in the direction of the back door. "You'll see," was all she would say.

Once outside, Leanne dug in her heels, slowing her mother's forward movement. Four men exited one guest cabin, two with moving dollies, and headed back toward their truck. "Mama, what is going on here?"

"You'll see," Joanna said cryptically.

Leanne had no choice, she had to go along.

It was amazing the difference in her mother after only one week of medication. She had more energy than she'd had in over a year. She was happy, always talking about the future and Dex.

Leanne pushed thoughts of him away. She would not think about him today.

Especially not today.

And now this.

Leanne tried to muster up some enthusiasm for her mother's benefit. She hated to be depressed when her mother was so obviously getting her life back. But she just couldn't help it.

"We are ready!" Joanna announced as she dragged Leanne into the first guest cabin.

Leanne gasped. The cabin was fully furnished with a queen-size bed, dresser and mirror, couch, two chairs, and a dinette set that seated four. It was beautiful. It was everything she'd dreamed it would be. But the bank had turned down her request for a start-up loan. How was this possible? How could this be?

Dex.

Leanne cried. She just couldn't help herself.

Her mother wrapped her arms around her. "Don't cry, child." She hugged her close. "He only did it because he loves you."

"He doesn't love me," Leanne wailed. "He lied to me!"

"Shhh. I know he didn't tell you the truth and he should have." She rubbed Leanne's back affectionately. "But deep down you knew all along."

She had known, Leanne admitted. She'd known he was different somehow…

"He's called you every day. Even come by a couple of times and you won't even hear him out."

Leanne swiped at her eyes. "How can I believe anything he says now?"

"Look at it from his point of view," her mother coaxed. "Look how much courage it took for him to come here and face the past…come to terms with who he is." She shook her head. "He didn't come here to hurt you—or to fall in love with you. But he did."

Leanne sniffed. "You don't know that he loves me."

Her mother smiled. "Yes, I do," Joanna said softly. "I'm not sure he fully understands exactly what he feels yet, but he loves you."

Leanne gathered her composure. "Well, he's got a funny way of showing it."

Her mother winked. "If my intuition is right, and it usually is, you ain't seen nothing yet. Now come along, we have to get all gussied up."

Leanne frowned. "What?"

Joanna curled her arm around Leanne's. "We're going to that shindig at the Circle C today."

Leanne stopped dead in her tracks. "I can't do that. I can't possibly face him."

"I've been cooped up in that house for over a year now. Would you begrudge your dear old mother a day of festivities?"

Leanne admitted defeat. How could she possibly deny her mother? She couldn't.

She would just have to face him. She prayed with all her heart that her mother was right—that Dex did love her. Because she was madly, foolishly in love with him.

Two hours later, her heart pounding like a drum, Leanne parked her old truck in the Coopers' crowded drive. It looked as if the whole community was there already. Anxiety threatened to shatter her bravado.

Firming her shaky resolve, Leanne walked to the backyard with her mother. Joanna was immediately swept into the crowd of friends and neighbors who were glad to see her out and about. Leanne waited on the fringes of the gathering, scanning faces for the person every fiber of her being ached to see.

Then she saw him.

Her gaze moved over him hungrily. The fit of his jeans, the way his broad shoulders filled out his white shirt. His wind-tousled hair. She smiled. He hated wearing a hat, she realized suddenly. That's why he was always forgetting it.

Dex was talking to his Grandfather Cooper, who'd been released from the hospital two days ago. Thankfully, Mr. Cooper was going to be fine. Medication and proper exercise were going to keep his condition under control.

Dex smiled at something his grandfather said. Leanne's heart reacted in its usual manner. How could she have thought that she could spend the rest of her life without ever seeing that smile again, without kissing those lips?

She couldn't. She simply couldn't.

Now, if only her mother's intuition would prove correct...

One-thirty. Dex's shoulders sagged. The Montgomerys weren't going to come.

He should have known. He'd expected too much

too soon, he supposed. He shook his head. He just
wanted his family together, where they belonged.

He'd been sure his ultimatum would work, but why
should it? It hadn't worked for his father more than
thirty years ago.

A strong hand clapped Dex on the back. "Don't
look so down and out, brother," Ty told him. "They
could still come."

"I'm not so sure."

Ty squeezed his shoulder. "I am. I saw something
change in the old man while I was there." He
shrugged. "It was like all the little differences he noticed in me made him think about the grandchild he'd
walked away from all those years ago."

Grandfather Cooper's words echoed in Dex's ears.
He'd said virtually the same thing.

"I hope you're right," Dex offered.

"Boys." Grandmother Cooper hugged Dex, then
Ty. "I just have to tell you one more time how proud
I am to have you together at last."

Grandfather Cooper appeared and kissed his wife's
cheek. "We're all proud." The happiness in his eyes
punctuated his words. "We're finally complete now."

"Your mother and father would be proud of you
both," Grandmother Cooper told them, emotion shining in her eyes.

"That means a great deal to me," Dex said hum-
bly. This was as close as he would ever get to knowing what his mother was like.

Ty elbowed him and nodded toward the far end of
the crowd. "You've got company, bro."

Dex followed his gaze.

Leanne.

She was beautiful. Wearing that same white dress she'd worn the first time they made love, she looked like an angel straight from heaven. At that instant Dex knew that everything in his mixed-up life would be right if only he could convince her to forgive him.

Determined to make it happen, he excused himself and strode straight up to her. She looked ready to run. "Just give me three minutes." He took her by the arm, a jolt of awareness instantly searing him. "That's all I ask of you."

"All right," she said warily.

Dex led her away from the party. He paused a few feet from the barn, far enough away that they wouldn't be interrupted. He stared deeply into her eyes and told her the truth.

"When I came here it was more out of curiosity and maybe a little taste of revenge than anything else. I expected to resent these people, to be bitter about what they'd done to me." He slid his hand down her arm to grasp her hand. He didn't miss the little hitch the move elicited in her breathing. "But a couple of things happened while I was here. While I was pretending to be Ty I fell in love with these people."

Her big blue eyes peered up him, so full of hope yet still guarded. Though he could see the questions in her eyes, she waited for him to finish.

"The other thing is…" He squeezed her hand. "…Well, whether you can understand it or not, you saved me from the man I'd become. You showed me there was more to life than I ever imagined." He swallowed back the lump of emotion forming in his throat. "I fell in love with you. And if you can forgive me…"

She started to speak but he shushed her with a finger against those luscious lips. "I'd like very much if you'd agree to be my wife."

Leanne threw her arms around him. They held each other for awhile.

She finally drew back. "I love you, Dex," she said softly. "I love you so much. But I'm afraid that I won't fit into your world. We're so different...and I've got the dude ranch and my mother..." She shrugged. "I just don't see how it could work." She shrugged again, uncertain. "And...and I want more than just to be a wife. I want to make my father's dream come true in a big way."

He'd already thought of this. "We'll hire an assistant to help your mother run the dude ranch on a daily basis. We'll commute back and forth regularly." He smiled as he watched her eyes grow wider with hope. "Plus, I've talked to a friend of mine about forming a corporation that would set up dude ranches all over the state, maybe even in some others. You'll be the senior partner. You can run it any way you want." Before she could speak, he continued, "And you don't have to worry about fitting into my world." He cupped her face in his hands and kissed her, just the barest brushing of lips. "You *are* my world."

Tears slipped down her soft cheeks, but she smiled in spite of them. "In that case, then the answer is yes."

Dex escorted his bride-to-be over to his grandparents and made the formal announcement. He also introduced her to Ty's fiancée, Dr. Jessica Stovall from Atlanta. Everyone in the family had welcomed her with open arms when she arrived with Ty earlier in the week. Dex had never seen people go to such lengths to make another person feel wanted. They loved Jessica the moment they laid eyes on her. Since she had no family of her own, this was even more thrilling for Jessica. If only the Montgomerys would feel that way. Deliberately pushing that thought aside, happiness bloomed in Dex's chest as he watched Leanne welcoming Jessica into the family.

A hush abruptly fell over the crowd. The sound of a vehicle approaching drew his gaze to the driveway. A long black limousine parked only a few yards away. His heart skipped a beat when the door opened and his Grandfather Montgomery emerged from the elegant vehicle.

Grandfather Montgomery offered his hand to his wife as she emerged from the vehicle next, both of them looking the epitome of vogue and sorely out of place on this unpretentious Montana ranch. George, Dex's valet and confidant, climbed out next. They were all here.

Charles Montgomery, Senior, his wife on his arm, walked straight up to Wayne Cooper. For one long moment the two men simply stared at each other. Finally, Charles extended his hand and said so that all could hear, "I've been wrong about a lot of things for a very long time." He cleared his throat. "Worst of all, I hurt your family. I'd like to start fresh."

Wayne Cooper stood stock-still for three long beats, then he accepted the offered hand. "Nothing would please me more."

Grandmother Cooper hugged Grandmother Montgomery, tears of joy and relief flowing down their cheeks.

Dex hadn't realized until that moment that he was holding his breath. He exhaled raggedly. Finally, after all this time, things were right again.

"Holy smokes. Can you believe it?" Ty asked, stunned.

"I'm getting there," Dex murmured.

The Montgomerys approached Ty and Dex then. Dex found himself holding his breath all over again.

"Ty." Grandfather Montgomery nodded to Ty. "Dex." His gaze was bright with emotion. "I made a mistake thirty-three years ago. I was wrong and I've had to live with it all this time." He looked from Dex to Ty and back, then drew in a heavy breath. "I won't make the same mistake twice." He embraced each of his grandsons, then looked at them with pride beaming from his expression. "I can't believe the two of you are finally together." He shook his head. "I never allowed myself even to think this could happen." His voice wavered when he said, "Thank God I was wrong."

Dex hugged his Grandmother Montgomery as well. He was so glad to see them. She held on a moment longer when he would have pulled away.

She hugged Ty next, and murmured, "Thank you so much for having the courage to come to us." When she released him her own eyes were brimming with emotion. "And for making our family whole again."

Ty nodded, obviously too overcome to speak.

Dex put his arm around Leanne then. "This is Leanne Watley," he told the Montgomerys. "My fiancée." He wanted his family to love her as much as he did.

Another joyous round of hugs followed, accompanied by heartfelt congratulations. For the first time in his life, Dex felt right. Complete—whole, as his grandparents had said.

When the Coopers had ushered the Montgomerys over to meet some of their friends, George made his way to Dex.

"It's very good to see you, sir," George offered stiffly.

"Good to see you, too, George."

George looked him up and down. "I see you've been blending in with your environment."

Dex couldn't help a grin. "I have. Do you approve?"

A tiny smile twitched the reserved man's lips. "I most certainly do, sir. When in Rome..." He waggled his brows.

Dex, pride and love bursting inside him, ushered his fiancée forward a step. "This is Leanne Watley. We're getting married."

George gave her a thorough once over then gave Dex a nod of approval. "It's a pleasure, madam." He kissed Leanne's hand.

Before George could fathom her intent, she'd thrown her arms around him and hugged him. "Nice to meet you, too, George."

Startled, George cleared his throat when she released him. "Well, perhaps I should see to the Montgomerys' luggage."

Dex frowned. "Luggage?"

"According to their itinerary, they plan to stay the weekend." With that, George executed an about-face and went about his business.

"Dex."

He turned to Leanne, who made him want to take her in his arms just looking at her. "Hmmm?"

"Who's George?"

"I'll explain later. Right now—"

Dex's next words were interrupted by the easy bantering between the grandfathers over the best cut of beef.

"You might need this, brother." Ty paused beside him, offering a cold long-necked bottle of beer.

"I think you might be right," Dex agreed as he accepted the drink.

Ty held out his own bottle. "A toast," he suggested, "to the future."

"Hear, hear," Dex said as they clinked glass. He took a long swallow then turned to Leanne. "And to us," he murmured before kissing her lips.

Epilogue

One month later

Dex waited on the left side of the pulpit, Ty on the right. Both were dressed in similar black tuxedos, both waited expectantly to take the next step in the rest of their lives. Dex smiled when Ty's gaze caught his.

"Don't worry, she'll be here," Dex assured him upon noting the worry in his eyes.

Ty nodded. "I know."

Jessica had had to return to Atlanta to close down her practice and finalize other business affairs. Ty was scared to death that she was having second thoughts—especially after she'd called and said her flight had been delayed and she wouldn't be arriving until just before the wedding.

But she'd be here. Dex was sure of it. And, deep down, so was Ty.

A hush fell over the crowd assembled in the Rolling Bend Community Church as the wedding march sounded from the ancient organ. Angelica, looking like the princess she was, cantered down the aisle, throwing rose petals left and right. She paused at the pew where Jenny's twins sat then sprinkled the boys with pink petals. They giggled. Beaming, Angelica continued her enthusiastic journey toward the front of the church. When she stopped, she looked first at her Uncle Ty and grinned, then to her Uncle Dex and winked.

Dex felt sure she had some self-serving plan for him, but today he didn't care. He winked back. The little girl grinned.

Suddenly Leanne appeared at the far end of the long rows of polished wood pews. Pride filled him as Dex watched his bride, escorted by George, walk down the red-carpeted aisle toward him. The white wedding dress and veil only made her look more angelic, more beautiful. Dex wasn't sure his heart could tolerate the rush of emotions that surged through him.

Looking regal, George smiled as he left Leanne standing at Dex's side. They both looked back to see Jessica, accompanied by Dr. Baker, approach next.

Ty's sigh of relief was audible. Jessica looked stunning as well. Ty's eyes literally shone with the love burning inside him.

At last, Dex realized, everything was perfect.

The families were together with only the occasional colliding of egos. MOCO Enterprises, the name they'd given the Montgomery–Cooper beef venture, as well as the Wild W Dude Ranch Retreat, were off the ground and running.

And now, the icing on the cake…Leanne would be his.

It was all any man could hope for and more.

Before turning his attention to the minister, Dex

quickly surveyed the faces of his and Ty's family. All seated together, all smiling.

It didn't get better than this.

"Dearly beloved," the minister began.

"Dex!" Leanne whispered, leaning slightly toward him.

He eased a bit closer to her, a question in his eyes as he searched her uncertain ones. "Yes?" he whispered back.

"The stick turned blue."

"What?"

The word echoed through the chapel, startling the minister into silence.

"We're pregnant," she murmured, then chewed her bottom lip as if she feared his reaction.

He was going to be a father.

He was going to be a father! His eyes widened in disbelief. Startled, confused, and humbled, Dex smiled down at his beautiful bride. "Are you sure?"

She nodded.

Dex pulled Leanne into his arms and kissed her for all she'd given him, for making his life complete.

"What's going on?" someone asked in a stage whisper.

"Didn't ya hear?" Angelica demanded, turning to those seated behind her. "She said the stick turned blue! Just what we need around here—more babies. Ain't the one Uncle Ty and Aunt Jessica's gonna adopt enough?"

Ty leaned toward Dex and offered his hand. "Congratulations, brother."

Dex pulled his brother into an embrace. "I couldn't let you get ahead of me."

Ty drew back. "Yeah." Emotion shimmered in his eyes. "I knew you'd catch up."

As the enthusiasm spread through the church, Jessica hugged Leanne. "I'm so glad we'll be doing the mommy brigade together."

"Thanks, sis," Leanne said tearfully.

Dex felt as if he might break down and cry himself. Neither Leanne nor Jessica had siblings of their own—and he definitely knew how that felt. The two were like sisters now. Life truly was perfect.

Once the cheers and applause had died down, the minister continued with the double wedding ceremony.

Dex kissed his bride.

So did Ty.

And they all lived happily ever after.

Coming in December from

AMERICAN *Romance*®

and

Judy Christenberry

RANDALL WEDDING
HAR #950

Cantankerous loner Russ Randall simply didn't need
the aggravation of playing hero to a stranded
Isabella Paloni and her adorable toddler. Yet the
code of honor held by all Randall men wouldn't
allow him to do anything less than protect
this mother and child—even marry Isabella
to secure her future.

**Don't miss this heartwarming addition
to the series**

Brides
for Brothers

Available wherever Harlequin books are sold.

How to Marry A HARDISON

by Kara Lennox

continues this December in

HARLEQUIN®

AMERICAN *Romance*®

SASSY CINDERELLA

After an accident knocked him off his feet,
single dad Jonathan Hardison was forced to hire
a nurse to care for him and his children.
The rugged rancher had expected a sturdy,
mature woman—not Sherry McCormick,
the sassy spitfire who made Jonathan wish
their relationship was less than *professional*....

**First you tempt him.
Then you tame him...
all the way to the altar.**

Don't miss the other titles in this series:

VIXEN IN DISGUISE
August 2002

PLAIN JANE'S PLAN
October 2002

HARLEQUIN®
Makes any time special®

Visit us at www.eHarlequin.com

HARHTMAH3

These are the stories you've been waiting for!

Based on the Harlequin Books miniseries
The Carradignes: American Royalty comes

HEIR TO THE THRONE

Brand-new stories from

KASEY MICHAELS

CAROLYN DAVIDSON

Travel to the opulent world of royalty with these two
stories that bring to readers the concluding chapters in
the quest for a ruler for the fictional country of Korosol.

Available in December 2002 at your favorite retail outlet.

HARLEQUIN®
Makes any time special ®

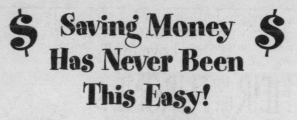

$ Saving Money $ Has Never Been This Easy!

Just fill out and send in this form from any October, November and December 2002 books and we will send you a coupon booklet worth a total savings of $20.00 off future purchases of Harlequin and Silhouette books in 2003.

Yes! It's that easy!

I accept your incredible offer!
Please send me a coupon booklet:

Name (PLEASE PRINT)

Address   Apt. #

City   State/Prov.   Zip/Postal Code

In a typical month, how many
Harlequin and Silhouette novels do you read?

❏ 0-2   ❏ 3+

097KJKDNC7   097KJKDNDP

Please send this form to:
In the U.S.: Harlequin Books, P.O. Box 9071, Buffalo, NY 14269-9071
In Canada: Harlequin Books, P.O. Box 609, Fort Erie, Ontario L2A 5X3

Allow 4-6 weeks for delivery. Limit one coupon booklet per household. Must be postmarked no later than January 15, 2003.

HARLEQUIN®
Makes any time special®

Silhouette
Where love comes alive™

Steeple Hill Books is proud to present
a beautiful and contemporary new look
for Love Inspired!

As always, Love Inspired delivers
endearing romances full of hope, faith and love.

Beginning January 2003
look for these titles
and three more each month
at your favorite retail outlet.

Steeple
Hill®

Visit us at www.steeplehill.com   LINEW03